HOW TO TAME TRICKSTER FAE

A COZY MONSTER ROMANCE

WILD OAK WOODS

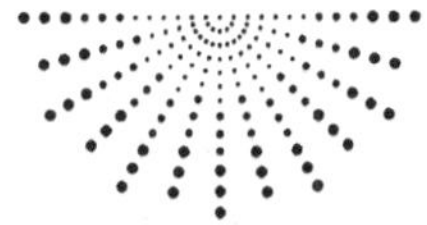

JANUARY BELL

HOW TO TAME A TRICKSTER FAE

AUTHOR'S NOTE

The stakes will be low, the spice will be hot, and the men will be monstrous— but only in the best ways.

For a full list of content warnings and an introduction please visit the Wild Oak Woods website.

CHAPTER ONE

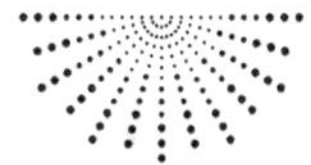

My hands curl around the bone china, the thin cup doing almost nothing to protect the skin of my fingers from the heat of the near-boiling tea. A rose petal bobs at the surface, a lavender bud following in its wake from where they've escaped the copper tea strainer.

I close my eyes, inhaling the aroma deeply, trying to ground myself in this moment, with this tea I've been saving for just this occasion.

The letter sits atop a lace napkin on the table beside me, all of which shakes nervously with the rhythm of my leg jangling against the floor. Closed with a red wax seal embossed with a diamond sigil that makes my heart beat all the faster.

The mark of the Enchanter's Lapidary and Metalsmithing Guild.

"Only the premiere organization for jewelry enchanters," I tell Fenn. He's curled up on the hearth, the embers of this morning's fire still burning softly in the grate.

Fenn ignores me, as he usually does, his fluffy red tail flicking slightly in annoyance at the fact I've had the audacity to disturb his nap.

Having a nocturnal familiar can be incredibly trying.

"Maybe I should go next door and open the letter with Piper there," I muse.

It's not talking to yourself if your familiar is around. That's an unwritten rule of witchery, I'm sure of it.

This time, though, Fenn raises his fluffy red head and blinks slowly at me.

"You think that would be a good idea?" A shoulder to cry on or a friend to celebrate with—either way, Piper will know the perfect thing to say.

If it's another rejection, I can get a cupcake.

If the guild has finally come to their senses and decided to extend me an offer of membership, I can *also* get a cupcake.

Either way, there is a frosted confection in my future, and that heartens me. A little, at least.

Mostly, though, I'm a bundle of nerves and excitement and trepidation.

"Do you want to come with me?" I ask Fenn.

He lets out a whiny yip in response, then bundles closer into himself.

"It's an early morning for me, too," I say, amused at my little fox familiar's annoyance at me.

We keep late hours, in general, working the shop below our snug apartment in the late mornings for the few customers that come through my doors. In-person clientele are rare, brought in by the little word of mouth that gets out of Wild Oak Woods into the larger world, though we do a bustling mail-order business that keeps the lights on and food on the table.

Fenn and I have spent many lazy afternoons together, leafing through spell books in the sun-soaked window seats and slowly going through the massive inventory left to me by the former owner of Witchwork's Jewelry. Evenings and late nights are best for spellwork and crafting enchanted rings, the highest in demand, and he's there with me too, watching and lending energy where he can, my little magic fox battery and companion.

"It's a good life we have," I tell Fenn, and it is—I know I'm lucky. I know it.

But it's a lonely life, despite the network of witches in town, my new friends. I love my work, but without the recognition from the damned guild…

I sigh, tracing my finger over the wax seal.

Fenn yips again, not even bothering to move his tail.

"I'll bring you back something," I tell him. My teacup rattles on its saucer as I set it down, gone cold while I brooded.

Fenn whines, my vocal little familiar voicing his strong fox opinions.

"Two somethings," I amend. He rewards me by fluffing his tail and curling up into an even tighter ball.

I raise an eyebrow and huff a laugh, stuffing the letter in the pouch on the belt around my favorite green linen dress.

It takes no time at all to lock the door to my little apartment, the heavy key hanging on a long chain around my neck, and I make my way down the back stairs, avoiding going into the storefront at all, as if walking by my spare jewelry displays will jinx the contents of the letter.

My pulse picks up as the morning sun caresses my skin, and I slip into the back of The Pixie's Perch, dodging the grumpy troll line chef who grunts at me in annoyance as I squeak through the door into the bustling dining room.

The bakery counter has a line that winds out the front door, full of perfect pastries in shades of pastel.

The morning rush.

"There she is," Piper crows in delight, her pretty brunette hair tied back in a complex crown of braids. A pink ribbon's laced through it, and she looks perfectly in place here, in her domain, surrounded by sweets and pastries chock-full of magical effects.

Muttering niceties, I squeeze through the crowd to the table she stands at.

"Oh," I say, my heart fluttering.

They're all here. Well, most, at least, of the witches of Wild Oak Woods, gathered around the table with expectant expressions. A three-tiered treat stand overflows with chocolate-filled pastries and tiny sandwiches, a pot of steaming coffee on a quilted pad next to it.

"You're all here."

Piper cringes slightly before bestowing me with a wide smile. "We knew you might need us." She takes a pink frosted cupcake from the stand and places it on a thin china plate embellished with deer and flowers, and I swallow hard as she slides it in front of the chair.

"Sorry," Rosalina says, her hands twisting anxiously in her long brown hair. "Squeak told me you had big news coming." The mouse in question, her familiar, pokes its whiskered nose from Rosalina's apron pocket. "We thought it would be best if we were here for you."

I look around at the five witches, my friends, and my heart aches.

"Thank you," I say softly, sinking into the empty seat at the table. "This is…"

"We're your friends, like it or not," Nerissa says crisply.

Willow snorts at the spellsmith's customary bluntness, but the healer squeezes my hand across the table. "There's no magic like—"

"If you say the power of friendship, I will throw a cucumber sandwich at you," Nerissa tells her sourly, flipping her blue-black hair over one shoulder.

"I was going to say the power of a coven, but you interrupted me." Willow glares at her.

"We're not a coven," Rosalina cautions. "You shouldn't say that. You never know who's listening. We would have to have a charter, and get approval, and sanctioned, and—"

"Squeak is probably listening," Nerissa interrupts, jerking her head at the whiskers still sticking out of Rosalina's pocket. "We all know the biggest gossip here is the one who gets it from the rest of our familiars."

Squeak pops more fully out, chittering angrily at Nerissa.

I snort in amusement, which draws everyone's attention back to me.

"Well, open it," Piper urges, making a hurry-up motion with a flour-dusted hand.

I fish the envelope from the pouch on my belt, straightening a slightly crumpled corner. My heart seems to stand still in my chest, my anxiety ramping up.

"I didn't plan on reading this in front of an audience," I tell them grimly.

"It could be a yes," Piper says. That's Piper, though—she's unfailingly positive no matter what. The pink ribbon trailing from her hair bobs as she nods in agreement with herself.

Nerissa shoots me a look of understanding, and that, more than anything, tightens my throat. Nerissa is more than a spell-smith—she dabbles in darker shadow magic, in things Piper and the rest of us wouldn't dream of touching.

She has what my mother would have called 'the knowing,' and right now, I'm not sure I like that about her at all.

The envelope tears slightly as I pull away the red wax seal, and the breath whooshes out of me as I read it quickly.

Dear Ms. Wren Tierson,

We regret to inform you that your application to the Enchanter's Lapidary and Metalsmithing Guild has, yet again, been denied. We have, in fact, made note of all eleven of your failed applications, and while your work is impressive for a witch who has been cast out from their coven, we would be ill-advised to accept such an applicant.

We wish you well in your pursuits, and if you would like to purchase additional correspondence courses and materials, we are more than happy to provide them.

Best wishes,

The Enchanter's Lapidary and Metalsmithing Guild

"WELL?" Rosalina prompts, the mouse in her pocket staring at me with glossy black eyes. "What does it say?"

"By the crone," Nerissa says crabbily, "use your eyes. She's been rejected again."

I want to glare at Nerissa, but the pretty raven-haired witch is entirely right. I settle for staring at my hands instead.

"They said not to apply again. Pretty much." My throat is tight, and I can barely force the words out. I pour myself a cup of black coffee, wishing I'd stayed upstairs in my little apartment where I could snuggle Fenn and cry in privacy.

"What?" Piper's face is astounded, her eyes wide and mouth a thin line of annoyance. "How dare they?"

"They don't want an outcast." The word is bitter on my tongue. "Without a coven, they won't even look at my application."

Nerissa glares daggers at the open letter before me. I drink the coffee just to have something to do, and it's too hot and strong and overwhelming after the bad news.

My shoulders sag in disappointment, and I fight the wave of self-pitying tears that threaten. "I needed this," I say, flapping the letter at the four witches in front of me. "I need to be in their good graces."

I set my jaw, more obsessed than ever with getting into the goddess-damned guild one way or another.

"I'll figure out a way in," I grind out. "I'll be so good they can't ignore me."

Piper gives me a bleak look. "You're already the best enchantress we've seen."

"That's not saying much," Nerissa snarks.

Willow laughs again, but the healer watches me carefully. "We could start our own coven. Then you could try again."

I shake my head, mustering a placating smile that doesn't stretch to my eyes. "You know no one wants anything to do with me. The Elder Council won't touch anything I'm a part of. Not after…" I trail off, and the rest of the women around the table pick up the conversation, discussing how, exactly, they could begin their own coven here in Wild Oak Woods.

I stew in my thoughts and pick at the cupcake in front of me, Piper's signature pleasure spell woven into the frosting hardly touching my black mood.

Until the door of The Pixie's Perch blows open, a gust of chilly air sending the chimes above it tinkling. The five of us whip our attention to it, the faint fingers of magic sending the hair on the nape of my neck upright.

A birch-branch broom just inside the pastry shop falls to the black and white tiled floor with a clatter, and I jump.

"Change is on the wind," Nerissa says darkly. "Company is coming."

Piper and Willow exchange a look, concern furrowing their brows.

The preternatural stillness vanishes as suddenly as it arrived, and the whole of The Pixie's Perch seems to shake itself as business resumes at the same fever pitch like nothing happened.

Something happened, though.

Change is on the wind.

CHAPTER TWO

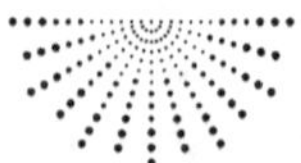

CAELAN

I'm in a foul mood. Kieran is likewise in a foul mood, though that's nothing new. The Unseelie prince scowls as he surveys the fish charring over the fire.

Only Ga'Rek seems to be enjoying our so-called jaunt outside of the Underhill.

Better here than in Her Majesty's dungeons, though.

I cast a sidelong glance at Kieran. The prince has never been outside the palatial halls and luxuriously appointed rooms of the Underhill's palace. Even as the fourth spare to the throne, the fae prince was spoiled rotten by his doting mother and all the two-faced courtiers hoping to score her favor.

Sighing, I turn my own fish over the fire.

Might as well get both sides evenly burnt.

Ga'Rek hums under his breath, and Kieran skewers him with a look the huge half-orc changeling is only too happy to ignore.

"If I didn't know better, I'd say you were happy to be out of the Underhill," I say, finally giving up on an even char on the damned trout and popping a piping hot piece in my mouth. It's not bad.

It's real, at least, not the sawdust the Queen would be making us eat as prisoners of her magic beneath the palace.

A shiver goes through me.

"Why wouldn't I be?" The orc squares his shoulders, sizing me up. "Would you rather be rotting in her dungeons?"

Kieran sighs, and I immediately roll my eyes at the now-familiar sound.

"I was just defending myself," he says, and there's a petulant whine to the comment that sets my teeth on edge.

It's what he's said, over and over and over again, since the night he nearly gutted his eldest brother and heir to the throne.

It is *true*, which is the only reason, I suspect, we were allowed by Her Dark Majesty to escape to the above world, to the mortal realm, several days ago.

Days, which are still a strange concept, still feel odd, even though I've been topside before, to wreak havoc and mischief on the mortals who live here.

I am used to the endless dark of the Underhill, of the Queen's black moods and midnight predilections.

Even now, though, I can feel her presence, a dark shape in the shadows of the trees around us, though it's weaker now, during daylight hours.

Maybe Kieran's words aren't the only thing rubbing my nerves raw.

"Fish is good," Ga'Rek says, grinning broadly at me, his tusks gleaming in the small daytime fire.

"Better than sawdust and bonemeal," Kieran says wearily, echoing my own thoughts. "What was I supposed to do, let him kill me?"

I want to stab the pointy stick in my hand through his royal eye, but I grit my teeth and keep the urge to myself.

Kieran, for all his faults, is my friend.

"You survived."

"Why do you say that like it's my fault?" he asks.

"Well, technically, it is your fault. This is all your fault. But you made the choice to live, so now we have to deal with it." I shrug one shoulder, the stiff leather jerkin creaking slightly. "You can either drive us all crazy by repeating the same drivel over and over again, or you can shut up and decide to make the best of it."

"That's no way to speak to a prince." He sounds completely mortified.

Ga'Rek bursts out laughing, and a flock of birds scatter overhead in terror. "You're not the prince of shit anymore, Kieran. You can either be a dead prince or a living outcast. I know what I'd prefer if I were you."

He sniffs, clearly annoyed with both of us but unable to argue.

"This is a good place," Ga'Rek announces. "Besides, I know of somewhere for us to live. For a time, at least."

If they think we'll be in the Dark Queen's good graces and allowed to return to the Underhill again anytime soon, they are sorely mistaken. I am saved from voicing the thought by our much-maligned fae Prince.

"What, in some hollowed-out tree with a bullfrog for company?" Kieran snipes. His bright green wings scrabble against each other, the buzzing a sure sign of his annoyance.

I resist the urge to stab him. Truly, good for me.

"Why?" Ga'Rek smiles even wider. "Did you find one?"

I burst out laughing. Ga'Rek was dealt a shit hand by the fae, taken as a child from his orc family and given fae strength and longer life in return for his service to the Crown.

It didn't change him, though. He's remained as steadfast and kind as he was as a child.

I should know, since I was the one that took him.

"There's a village over that hill," Ga'Rek finally says, jerking his chin over his shoulder. "At least, there was when I was child. I remember it well."

Kieran scoffs. "When you were a child? That could have been three hundred years ago in mortal time."

"Maybe. Maybe it's gone." He shrugs a shoulder, though there's a hint of sadness around his eyes. "Maybe we can still find something worth salvaging there. A place to seek refuge, shelter, at the very least."

My skin prickles, the tops of my ears tingling.

There's magic at work here.

It's not the Dark Queen's either.

The unfamiliar rub of it sends goosebumps prickling across my purple skin, and I squint into the distance, where my fae sight can just make out the merry puffs of smoke in the distance.

The perfume of magic, I think, comes from there.

Exactly where Ga'Rek seemed to think there would still be a village.

"We should go," I say, stabbing the fish on a stick into the ground and rubbing my hands together. "I do *so* love mortals. A good plan, 'Rek."

He grins at me before taking my abandoned fish and swallowing the rest whole.

Kieran just looses a long-suffering sigh, his iridescent beetle wings reflecting the sunlight.

🐚

"This is not what I remember," Ga'Rek chokes out, staring all around with a wide-eyed enthusiasm that's contagious. His tusks are on full display as he grins, clearly delighted with the flourishing mortal settlement.

Not just humans, either—I'm pleased to know I was right about the source of the magic tickling the tips of my ears.

There is magic here. Real magic, different than the illusions of the Dark Queen. It's a cat curling around my shins, butting its head against me for attention. It's so strong it's seeped into the cobblestones, which line the network of streets throughout the vibrant town.

"Wild Oak Woods," Kieran announces, his wings buzzing in their green casing. "Smells like witches."

"Smells like fucking pastries," Ga'Rek adds enthusiastically. "Smells *fucking* delicious."

I'm not sure if it's the heady mortal magic in the air or the scent of sugar and butter—but Ga'Rek is right.

It smells incredible, and tantalizing, and perfect, and I've never been one to deny any of my impulses.

That would go against my wicked Unseelie heritage. I wouldn't even dream of it.

"I like it." I inhale deeply, as if I can suck the very source of the incredible scent straight into my lungs.

The uneven cobblestone streets are impeccably clean, compared to the bigger mortal cities out east, and an absolute plethora of boutiques and restaurants and taverns crowd along the path. Each boasts glossy clear windows, expensive windows. I run the tip of my tongue over one fang, delighting in the excess. Colorful signage shouts out the wares in gilded lettering above striped awnings.

The streets aren't bustling, not now, at least, but with the wicker lanterns swaying in the gentle breeze above, I have a feeling these streets are fuller when daylight wanes.

Oh yes, I like this place very, very much.

"There is mischief to be made here," I declare.

"I want whatever is causing that smell." Ga'Rek's stomach growls in agreement, and even Kieran smiles slightly.

"We don't even know what kind of currency these mortals use."

I strain my eyes with the force it takes to keep from rolling my eyes at him.

Ga'Rek's tusks flash in the sunlight as his smile widens and he tosses me an amused look.

"That's not a problem."

Kieran mutters something not worth hearing under his breath, and I shove my hands into the pockets of the leather vest and saunter down the street.

Firefly Lane, a signpost reads.

"How positively quaint," I say with admiration. I barely recollect this place. Then again, I've hardly ever been topside since snagging Ga'Rek as a strapping lad all those years ago.

Things have changed in a few hundred years, it seems.

Imagine that. The magic, for one, usually muted in this mortal place, is vibrant. Charged.

Wild. I fucking *love* it.

"It feels strange," Kieran, as always, is a thundercloud in a bright spot.

"Well, this is where we are making our home. For the time being, at least," I tell him with a hint of snarl. "So stop grousing and get that scowl off your face. You'll scare away all the good prey—mortals," I correct.

Not prey. No, no, that wouldn't do at all.

I whistle as we stroll, and then we're outside it: the source of the delicious scent of baked goods, of sugar and butter and all manner of sweet things.

"The Pixie's Perch," Ga'Rek intones, one dark, pierced eyebrow quirked at the sign overhead.

"I didn't know you could read," I announce, feigning shock.

His grin deepens. "That's because you're a rat bastard of the worst sort, who doesn't even care about his closest friend enough to know about his reading habits."

A pink and white striped awning blocks the afternoon sun, and we step closer to the small shop. Pastries line the window, arranged prettily with flowers to create some sort of wild-looking diorama. There's even a statue of a deer.

I bend closer. The thing is strangely lifelike, so real I could almost imagine its little white tail flicking this way and that.

Then it blinks, and I know I wasn't imagining it.

"A familiar," I breathe, slightly stunned. The deer disappears into the shop, and I follow it, entranced.

"A what?" Kieran asks Ga'Rek behind me.

A bell tinkles overhead, and sure enough, I scent it through the chocolate glazed eclairs and cinnamon shortbread and lavender-lemon scones.

Magic.

A witch's magic.

"Welcome to The Pixie's Perch," a lilting female voice sings out from the back room, and I smile. "Be right with you."

"This is it, lads." I turn to my companions, spreading my hands wide. "This is our new place. Among the witches of Wild Oak Woods."

Kieran pinches the top of his nose, his beetle wings buzzing in irritation.

As for Ga'Rek, he's staring, open-mouthed, into the small arched opening that must lead to the shop's kitchen.

And when the petite, pink-cheeked brunette human witch steps out, dusting her hands on her apron, I see the exact moment his life changes.

"You're outvoted, Kieran," Ga'Rek rumbles. "This is where we're staying."

A satisfied smile curls the corners of my lips as the witch pales, clocking exactly what we are in the span of a few seconds.

Her stunned reaction only lasts a moment before she's all smiles and rosy cheeks again.

"Well, we haven't had fae in town in... well, I don't know when," she babbles. "What can I do for you?" she asks.

"What's your name, pretty witchling?" I lean against the curved glass counter.

Ga'Rek growls at me in warning, and I suppress a laugh at his expense.

The witch, however, just blushes. "If you think I'll freely give you my name without knowing yours, you've got Wild Oak Woods all wrong." She arches an eyebrow and spreads her small hands wide. "What can I get you?"

A laugh hums behind me, Ga'Rek as clearly smitten with her as it is day outside.

"We are, as you've noticed," I pause for effect, glancing sidelong at Kieran's deep lavender skin and bright green beetle wings, "new here. Can you recommend a place for us to stay?"

"Change is on the wind," the witch mutters, her attention lingering a moment on a birch broom beside the door.

I follow her look, confused by her non-answer. Mortals are such strange creatures. Witches, though, are even stranger.

"Answer me this," she says. "Do you mean the citizens of our town harm? Do you come here for sport?" There's an icy ring of glass in the questions, some of her syrupy sweetness falling away.

"No," I answer, honestly, for once. "We seek refuge away from the Underhill."

Kieran's jaw drops, and even Ga'Rek gives me an annoyed look, his green brow pinched, huge ham hands fisting at his sides.

I do roll my eyes, now, and it feels glorious.

"From the Underhill," the witch repeats. In an instant, her icy demeanor melts, though concern still crinkles the corners of her eyes.

Kieran shifts on his feet, and Ga'Rek puts a massive hand on his still frenetically buzzing wing.

"Right." She nods once. "Well, you'll find Wild Oak Woods to be welcoming of strangers who are welcoming of it."

"You speak as though the place is alive," Ga'Rek says, leaning forward, surveying the small witch from head to toe.

"What place isn't?" she counters. "Now, sit down and I'll bring you bread and salt. We can go from there."

"Clever," I say in admiration. "Bread and salt with the Unseelie fae."

An old magic, but a classic. Freely offered bread and salt,

while not necessarily foolproof, as many fools have found, ensures we mean the shopkeep witch no harm, and will create a pact of sorts between us.

There are loopholes, but for now, I'll play her little witchling games.

The door breezes open again, the bell tinkling merrily, and my attention whips to the newcomer.

Another witch.

With delicate, high cheekbones, a small, pointy chin, thick full lips and grass-green eyes. A snarled mess of blonde hair hangs heavy down one shoulder, and those spring eyes are rimmed in red, as if she's been crying.

The tips of my ears tingle again, and this, this witch, I realize, is who I scented back in the forest.

She smells of dark places in the earth, of gemstones and gold and of the wildest magic I've felt in all my years.

I see her, and my heart stills inside my chest, and when it begins beating again, I don't feel the same, not at all.

"You," I breathe, my eyes wide.

A red fox pushes past her in the doorway, yipping at me.

Ga'Rek coughs noisily into one of his oversized hands, breaking the momentary spell as I memorize every angle of her pretty, witchy face.

Well.

Perhaps our visit topside to the mortal realm will bear more fruit than I imagined.

Perhaps this Wild Oak Woods was calling to us the whole time.

Something about the witchling in the doorway certainly sings to me.

CHAPTER THREE

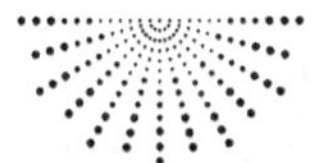

WREN

Three fae. Unseelie, judging by their lilac skin and icy eyes, except for the green one.

Fenn's darted past me, and I stare at the trio settling at one of Piper's tables in utter dismay.

Unseelie fae and an… orc? In Wild Oak Woods?

We have minotaurs and I'm pretty sure a vampire or two… an elf runs the boutique on the other side of my store, and a few shifters live in town as well… but a fae—an Unseelie at that— unheard of.

Two High fae from the Underhill.

My hands tremble slightly, and I shove them behind me.

"Aren't you a surprise." The male speaking hasn't so much as glanced away from me since I walked through the door of The Pixie's Perch, hoping for peace after the lunch rush and a pick-me-up pastry before I went back to inventorying gems.

I swallow hard.

He's beautiful, easily the most handsome man I've ever seen.

But beautiful in the way a too-sharp tool might be, all perfectly honed edges and dangerous in uncareful hands.

He'd cut, and deep, and you might not even feel it until you saw the blood.

That is, if anyone was foolish enough to let him too near.

I step closer, intrigued and slightly terrified.

"Who are you?"

Long black lashes flutter shut as he inhales deeply, before a wide smile stretches the corners of his mouth. It's a shade darker than the light purple of his skin, like he bit into a fresh blackberry and it stained it with a summery burst.

"Why, I could be your future, little love," he says, all cockiness.

A thick black vine of a tattoo crawls out from under the sleeve of his shirt, and I blink at it. Surely some trick of the light, or of his, but it looks like the tattoo marks are bleeding into existence while I watch.

A strange buzzing sounds, and my attention finally goes to the other fae, where the noise seems to be emanating from.

"Wings," the first one says through that razor-sharp smile. "That's what the noise is."

The orc makes a strangled sound, eyes as large as dinner plates—but he's not looking at me, no, he's staring openly at the black lines of the tattoo on the light purple fae's hand.

A moon and vines. I have no idea what it signifies, what it could mean to a fae who lives under the earth, no real moon to speak of.

"Bread and salt," Piper calls out, bustling towards the table from the kitchens. She stops in her tracks when she sees me. "Wren, what are you—" She cuts off the question with a sharp intake of air.

She's given them my name.

Names have power amongst the fae—especially in the Underhill.

Piper blanches.

"Wren," the tattooed fae purrs, pinning me in place with his pale, pale blue eyes, as clear as a cold spring. "A lovely name for a lovely witch."

I go hot and cold all over.

"Bread and salt," Piper repeats, jerking her head at me to sit, to join them. There's a bit of annoyance in her eyes, but she doesn't seem overly worried.

No, my pastry-making friend seems… completely fine.

There are two Unseelie fae sitting smack-dab in the middle of her adorable black and white patterned floor, their lavender and deep purple skin complementing the few pastel frosted cakes left under the glass counter.

The massive orc stands out like a sore thumb, and I can't help but notice the way he's watching her hungrily.

I don't think it's just for the honey-soaked loaf glistening on the platter in her hands.

The tattooed fae pushes one of the heart-backed chairs out with a toe, grinning at me as I warily sit beside him.

At least this ritual of bread and salt will give us a modicum of protection, and, with any luck, the ancient custom will protect the rest of our little village. Every muscle in my body's tense, and I focus on the serrated knife Piper expertly wields as she distributes a slice to each of the males at the table.

The men dwarf us, even the leanly muscled winged fae, and it's hard not to be painfully aware of their daunting physical presence.

Not to mention their innate magic, the citrus and smoke flavor of it tingling against my senses.

"I'm Caelan," the tattooed fae says after a perfunctory bite of the bread. "We appreciate your generosity."

The winged male makes a sound of slight disgust, a noise that turns into a muffled moan a second later as the orc spears him with a furious glance.

"I'm Ga'Rek," the orc offers after a beat, smiling broadly at

Piper, and then me. "As you've noticed, we're from the Underhill. We are hoping you know of a place we can stay here. Maybe some work."

Piper leans forward, her eyes glimmering with excitement. "As a matter of fact, I need help here. I need another set of hands in the kitchen."

"At the risk of sounding less than humble," the table groans, the platter of sliced bread sliding towards him as he puts his weight on it, "I am a fantastic cook."

Caelan arches an eyebrow, and the pressure of his attention finally flits away, towards the green-skinned orc. "Humility has never been one of your virtues, old friend."

"You would be the expert on that," Ga'Rek tells him cheerfully, and the two laugh uproariously at their shared inside joke, while the third fae sniffs at the bread before taking a delicate bite.

Piper clears her throat, wiping a crumb from her lips. "I don't have need of three bodies in my kitchen, though," she tells them apologetically. "Have you asked around anywhere else?"

Ga'Rek shakes his head, a smug look on his face as he studies the two fae with him. Caelan and the quiet, disdainful one who can't seem to manage an ounce of friendliness towards us.

I scoot further away from the table, and nearly scream in surprise when a warm arm stretches around the back of my chair.

Fenn chitters an angry warning at Caelan, who, sure enough, has put his arm around my chair. I lurch forward, caught between either moving closer to his arm or closer to the table and absolutely not wanting to touch him.

The *audacity*.

I settle for an uncomfortable position in the middle of the chair and skewering the presumptuous fae with a glare.

"Hmm. Isley, that's our town grocer, she might be short-handed, you could check there. She sells fresh fruit and vegetables on the square." Piper's gabbing away like this situation is entirely normal, like Unseelie fae are regulars in Wild Oak Woods.

It's silly, but it does relax me a little.

At the very least, I'm not moping about the guild's rejection. Well, I wasn't until I remembered it, the cold words of the letter hitting me all over again, a punch in the gut.

My eyes well with tears, and I hunch my shoulders. Fenn pushes his cold, wet nose against my ankle, his fluffy tail wrapping around my other leg. Caelan's watching me still, his pale eyes narrowed.

Piper claps her hands loudly and I inhale with a shudder, grateful she's pulled attention off the fresh tears. I wipe my fingers along my eyes, hoping no one's seen my distress.

"Isley is for sure where you should start. If nothing else, she can probably use the help getting her goods from farm to market. I think she was talking about starting a small restaurant too…" She keeps talking, but I'm only half-listening, trying to stop the angry tears that threaten.

I glance around, pleased to see two of the three are fixed on whatever Piper's saying.

Caelan, however, narrows his eyes at me, the smile that played along his lips disappearing as I dab at the stupid tears.

Mortified, I decide to ignore him completely.

He probably only wants to take advantage of whatever he perceives this weakness to be; he's probably just looking for a way in.

That's the Unseelie way. Bargains and tricks and promises they do everything in their power to keep the upper hand in.

I sit up ramrod straight. That won't be happening to me, thank you *very* much.

No matter how pretty their packaging, how compelling their story, I will not be taken in. Nope.

Though, I have to admit, upon closer inspection, the three seem a bit worse for wear.

Their clothes are rumpled, not polished finery, and there's a hunted look in their eyes. Maybe they really are just looking for a new place to live. Caelan in particular seems to be doing his best imitation of tired innocence, and the orc, though completely overwhelmingly huge, seems genuine enough.

"What about the apothecary?" I force myself to ask, unwilling to utter Willow's name. Last thing I need is to give these fae another name. Goddess only knows what they'd do with it.

My skin prickles at the knowledge they have mine.

"She could use some help finding some of the more rare herbs and—"

"Perfect," Caelan says quickly. "Perfect. The—" He clears his throat, pausing. "Kieran is excellent at finding things like that. It's in his nature." He says this as an aside to me, a conspiratorial slant to his smile.

I take another bite of the honey-sweet bread, staring him down as I chew meaningfully. See? I want to tell him. Bread and salt. You can't hurt me.

I don't trust you.

Kieran, the winged fae, buzzes in slight outrage, his cheeks turning a brighter purple.

"Don't deny it, Kieran," Ga'Rek says, putting a particular emphasis on the name. "You have a singular way with plants. The apothecary would be a good fit."

Kieran scowls at Ga'Rek, who just huffs a laugh and slathers a piece of bread with Piper's homemade butter, spiked with more honey—a spell for pleasant thoughts, if I know her.

And I do.

"And what do you do, witchling?" Caelan leans further forward, and I taste the scent of magic clinging to him.

I cant my head at him, annoyed with his presumptive tone, as well as the stupid nickname. "It's been a long time since I was a witchling. You already have my name, anyway."

"Well," he says the word slowly, positively beaming at me. "I might have your name, but I have better manners than to use it without your permission."

I glance at Piper, and she cringes slightly, nodding. Right. No help there.

"You can call me Wren," I say delicately. "Do you plan on doing something with my name, Caelan of the Underhill?" There's as much brave challenge in that question as I can muster.

I am a fantastic jeweler, a fact I take heart in despite the guild's rejection, and a great enchantress of jewels and metals.

But there's not much in my witchy arsenal that would be effective against this man—a fact I'm all too aware of at the moment.

"Wren," he says slowly, dragging the syllable out in a way that makes my heart flutter strangely. "I think you'll find that all I want to do with your name is speak it with pleasure."

I choke on my bite of bread, the rest of the table very studiously ignoring whatever in the world Caelan's just said to me.

It certainly shouldn't set me on fire from head to toe.

It certainly shouldn't send me to the point of distraction.

"I don't need help right now," I manage to croak.

"No, I suppose your type of work is solitary," Caelan continues, his icy lavender gaze pinning me in place. I can hardly breathe from the weight of it. "But if you need help, you know where to find me."

"Actually, no, I don't know where to find you." I snort, laughing a bit out of nerves and at the absurdity of this entire situation. Underhill fae. In my friend's bakery. In our small town, which is supposed to be my safe bubble away from the troubles of the outside world, and decidedly safe from the Unseelie.

Fenn, picking up on my distress, lets out his absolute worst ear-shattering howl.

There's nothing quite like a fox yowl to break the mood. I let myself smile, and I mean it, because I have no doubt my vocal familiar will stop whatever this fae's fixation on me is.

Caelan, however, simply leans closer, his nostrils flaring.

"You smell of the earth. Dark places. Precious metals. Magic." He tilts his head, that glossy, soft-looking black hair slipping from the knot at his neck. "I would like to help you, if you let me." His eyes meet mine, arresting and otherworldly beautiful.

"I, I—" I don't want to tell him no right now. Not with how he's looking at me, like I hung the moon itself, like finding dark places deep in the earth with him would be the best possible idea. "I don't need help at the moment."

"Then why are you so sad, pretty witch?" he murmurs the question so softly that I wonder if I've heard him correctly.

"The apothecary and Long Leaf Brews." She nods to herself "Those are your best bets. Ga'Rek, there's an inn at the end of Firefly Lane. You can find a set of rooms there while these two sort out their work. If you want to work with me, then I expect you here an hour before dawn," Piper, goddess bless her, interrupts, and I force my attention to her concerned face and concentrate on breathing.

Dark places with Caelan, as delicious as it sounds, would be very bad. I've never been good at relationships or men, and I would be more than out of my depth with the gorgeous fae.

Besides, I have my hands very full with work. My mouth twists to the side. At least, I have my hands full with trying to figure out how to build my business without the help of the guild.

Or the help of the coven that cast me out.

"You have my thanks and my sword," Ga'Rek tells her, interrupting my bleak thoughts.

Caelan appears distracted by Piper, too, but I can still feel his attention on me, a warm sort of awareness of him that sets me on edge.

Not that I'm ever not on edge.

"I have to go," I manage, tripping over the words. Fenn yips in agreement, trotting over to the door, tail held high.

"You know where to find me, if you change your mind," Caelan says, a knowing look creasing the corners of his eyes. "About help. Or anything else."

I make a non-committal noise, saved from replying by a pair of rowdy minotaurs breezing through the door. If I'd been asked who the largest men were in Wild Oak Woods this morning, the minotaur builder brothers would have taken the prize.

Next to Ga'Rek and the tall fae, though, they don't seem nearly as impressive.

I cough out a surprised laugh, practically running for the door. Their horns nearly graze the ceiling, and they stare in surprise at the fae and orc in our midst.

The chill afternoon air splashes across my hot cheeks as the door to The Pixie's Perch closes behind me. The birch broom on the side of the little shop rattles against the wall in the breeze, and I narrow my eyes at it.

Change has come to Wild Oak Woods, indeed.

Change, in the form of two Unseelie fae and their massive orc friend.

CHAPTER FOUR

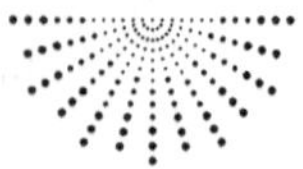

CAELAN

I whistle a tune to myself as I lean against the counter of the local apothecary shop, waiting for the witch they called Willow to appear.

The shop itself is a marvel of her witchcraft and her green thumb, and I have to admit the witch in question must be quite a talent.

My hands shake slightly, and I lace them together to hide it from Kieran, whose wings haven't stopped vibrating since the moment we walked in here.

I don't know how much my companions noticed when the stunning blonde enchantress walked into the syrupy-sweet bakery, but my heart hasn't stopped beating double time since I laid eyes on her.

Wren.

A witch.

After all these years, after days that flew into weeks and sprinted into months, a witch.

A witch!

My whistle goes sharp at the thought, and I tug at my sleeve, at the tattoo now vining across my skin.

The weight of Kieran's gaze drags across my arm, and I know he's seen it. I know he's seen the black edging along the purple of my wrist.

His wings buzz louder, and I grit my teeth at the noise.

How am I supposed to think straight with all that damnable noise?

"Oh!" We hear her before we see her, and to my surprise, Kieran stands up straighter, the high whine of his wings going blessedly, finally quiet as the witch, Willow, finally comes into view.

She's plump, a soft hourglass figure clothed in shades of emerald green to lovely effect, with glossy red-brown waves falling over one shoulder. Her hair's a flame against the greens of the many plants growing in every corner of the shop, hanging in gilded pots and stowed in wooden baskets.

There's even a thick wood bough over one table sprouting all manner of fungi, red-capped toadstools and white button mushrooms and a delicate yellow lace-type fungus I've never seen before.

"You are Willow?" Kieran asks, something like shock in his voice.

"You're an Unseelie fae," Willow responds, dusting her hands on a cream-colored apron. There's a bit of apprehension in her heart-shaped face, though her tone is clear and deliberate. "What brings you here? Who gave you my name?"

"Forgive us," I say, coming to my senses. "Piper and Wren sent us here. We are new in town, and looking for work."

Willow squints at me, then readjusts herself, standing straighter, though she is positively petite for a human and would be egregiously small for a fae.

Kieran clears his throat, and she zeroes in on him.

"You have beetle wings," she tells him.

He blinks, and I pinch the bridge of my nose as his wings begin to buzz again. Thank the sprites, though, he manages to pull them completely out, and Willow stands before him, her mouth agape, dazzled.

They iridesce in the sunlight streaming from the large circular-paned windows that make up the back wall of her store, and she closes her mouth with a snap.

"Well. Piper and Wren sent you? Are you just a pair of pretty wings or do you know your way around plants, fae?" She arches an eyebrow, her foot tapping beneath the hem of her dress. "Are you good with customers? Will you get in my way?"

Kieran makes a sound of consternation in his throat, his wings drooping slightly at her barrage of questions.

I bite my cheeks to keep from laughing.

I like this witch, too.

Perhaps our jaunt above the Underhill will be good for Kieran.

As soon as I set eyes on my Wren, I knew it would be for me. I smile to myself.

"He's been trained in all manner of plant lore," I say for Kieran, deciding this is where the princeling needs to be—with a plump and pretty flame-haired witch who will put him in his place. "He can be moody, but he aims to please."

The witch levels a look at me. "Does he speak for himself?" she asks tartly.

"I am at your service," Kieran says in a low voice, surprising me by sketching an equally low bow.

His wings extend again as he straightens, and a pink flush rides across Willow's cheeks.

"It won't be easy," she warns. "I have snapping kaninduelas in need of repotting, the gnarburls are about to bloom, and I need to harvest the crostrein nuts."

I raise an eyebrow at Kieran, waiting for him to shirk any

duties, especially those involving snapping kaninduelas, but he simply dips his head at her requests.

"I might have questions about how to do it to your standards, my lady," he says, all noble fae.

I roll my eyes and bite back a laugh. Either he's decided to accept fate's hand across his princely cheeks or he, too, has found a bossy little witch he likes.

Well, either way, it will make my life easier.

"Have fun," I say, breaking the staring contest between the two. "I'll head to Isley's… farm stand, is it?"

"She doesn't need help. She won't take yours, at least." The witch doesn't even look up at me, and my ego smarts a bit from all the attention she's lavishing on Kieran. Ah well, the young fae prince has always been short on attention from women.

Maybe this will do him some good, after all.

Although it is definitely not the kind of good the Dark Queen would approve of.

Which means it's the exact kind of thing I approve of… at the moment, at least.

"Where do you suggest I find work then, Willow witch?" I ask, stepping back as a strange flower begins to bud next to me. I watch it warily, putting space between the bloom and me and feeling the whisper of her verdant magic all around.

"Long Leaf Brews," she answers shortly, finally glancing at me. "The elf who owns it is welcoming of all manner of species… and she will probably be your best bet. Besides, she's busy with her new husband at the moment and could use some time off."

I wait, hoping she'll drop more hints that might help me get my way.

Not that I need help, but I do like to have an advantage when possible.

"You won't get her name from me," Willow says smartly, pulling a pair of glistening shears from her apron pocket. "Now go on, I don't need two of you scaring off clients. One with wings is enough. You come with me." She crooks a finger, and to my shock, Kieran follows without a look back.

I take a moment to glance around her strange, bewitching apothecary once more, avoiding the now blooming flower that seems to be leaning towards me, before making my way back outside.

Dusk's fallen, and I doubt Long Leaf Brews, whatever that may be, will be open for much longer.

An elf, a whole bustling coven of witches, the minotaurs... this is a strange place full of strange folk.

A fast clip-clop grows louder, and I dodge out the way as a huge male centaur with feathered hooves trots down the cobblestone street.

I should go find this elf and her new husband and make myself appealing to them.

Instead, I find myself following the muscled back of the dapple-grey centaur, back to The Pixie's Perch... and more importantly, back to the store next to it.

A jewelry boutique, fit for a metalsmithing witch with unkempt blonde hair and a wicked sharp gaze. Gold and silver gleam in the waning light, the last fingers of sunset setting the rare stones ablaze through the window.

Witchwork's Jewelry, a wooden sign overhead proclaims.

I drink it in, the lovely craftsmanship she's wrought on full display in the window. The magic chimes gently in the air, even through the glazed windows, the knack of her power compelling even without the stunning work on navy velveteen pillows.

Now that I know she's here, this blonde Wren, this little golden magpie of a witch, I will be hard-pressed to let her go.

My lips purse, and I begin to whistle tunelessly again.

The compulsion to pursue prey is as natural to my kind as breathing.

And Wren, the lovely, ethereal blonde enchantress, would make perfectly pleasant prey.

I smile to myself as she appears in the back of the shop, her strange brass magnifying glasses perched on her eyes as she works at a jewelry bench. I can barely make out the pink tip of her tongue as she concentrates, her red fox familiar curling around her ankles.

Even from here, I scent her—that rare perfume of deep, dark places in the earth, of gold and magic. Of power... and maybe something even better.

I shove my hands in my pockets and my grin broadens.

Yes, catching this little bird will be an excellent diversion from the nasty business of our exodus from the Underhill.

Now I just have to find out what will make her fly to me for help.

CHAPTER FIVE

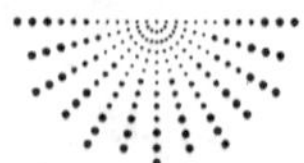

CAELAN

The urge to act on my needs pricks beneath my skin, annoying and persistent. The humid, late summer weather doesn't do much to alleviate the compunction. In fact, it only succeeds in making me all the more irritable.

The stairs to the old inn on groan on the way up to the patio.

It's a wonder the whole place hasn't rotted through.

Hash Beauchamp, the crotchety old owner of the place, rocks in a chair and watches me under fuzzy white eyebrows.

It's a wonder he's still alive, from the looks of him, matching the inn in both ambiance and cleanliness.

Which is to say, an extreme dearth of both.

I inhale slowly as Hash gives me a long look, pursing his lips in disapproval… and immediately regret it. The foul and unmistakable odor of wet dog—a noxious scent that permeates the entire place— nearly knocks me off my feet.

"You know, for a creature that's hardly fifteen pounds," I pause, lifting an eyebrow, "though he should be closer to ten, it seems, that dog has a way of truly infesting this place with smell."

The dog in question looks through rheumy eyes at me from his perch on Hash's lap. Pale brown splotches add to the filthy effect of the overweight and bug-eyed creature, and drool drips from his poorly aligned jaws.

It's so ugly it is quite nearly cute.

Hash should be offended at having the thing so close to his person. Alas, humans never were clever creatures.

Instead, the old man grins at me, roguish enough that it settles some of my persistent need to cause chaos, and jerks his head at the rocker next to him.

He should be offended, and yet, the more surly I behave towards him, the more he seems to like me.

I sigh in resignation and take the proffered chair.

"Does it not bother you?" I ask, setting my feet on the decaying wood porch and wrinkling my nose as I begin to rock.

"Having people stay at home? Or having an ugly purple fae on my porch?" He regards me curiously.

I snort, amused in spite of myself. Truly, not a clever man. A smart human would think better than to insult me, no matter how far I've fallen.

"How disgusting that creature smells," I say, looking pointedly at the rheumy dog in his lap.

The dog's tongue lolls out, more drool dropping onto the wooden floor.

No wonder it's mildewed.

"The entire inn stinks of him," I say, and something about that… there's something about that I should make note of, but then Hash grins at me, and I forget whatever it was.

"Good thing my sense of smell isn't as good as a fae's then, hmm, Purple?"

I roll my eyes, settling more deeply into the rocker. "Perhaps," I admit.

"You know, this old place has stood here for generations," he says. The floor of the porch shakes slightly as I rock forward, and my lip curls as I look around for any imminent signs of collapse.

All I see is a veritable family reunion of spiders in the corner. Charming.

"I would have never guessed," I tell him drily.

My rudeness does nothing to dissuade him, but it does put me in a slightly better mood.

"It's been here as long as I can remember," he says.

"Well, considering you were likely birthed on this very porch, I fail to be impressed,"

He laughs again, a sound that makes him seem much younger.

I narrow my eyes at him, the sense of strange… *wrongness* growing slightly.

Then the dog lets out a truly incredible belch, and I'm forced to look away again. Foul beast.

"That means he likes you," Hash says mildly.

"What, nearly regurgitating his dinner is a sign of approval?" I can't help but laugh at the absurdity of it.

"Mmhmmm."

This late in the day, the fireflies begin to dance around the edge of the Ever Forest, blinking in warm yellows through the thick wall of flowering brambles. There's something… something about the edge of the forest here.

"They say something lives in those woods," Hash tells me, following my attention.

"Well, yes, I'm sure it's full of bugs and other nasty little devils."

"You would be the authority on that, Purple," Hash says, and I bark out a laugh in surprise.

"I would indeed."

"I noticed a few of your tricks, too. Don't think I didn't. I'm old, but I'm not stupid."

"According to whom?" I ask.

He just laughs. The dog rolls onto it's back, and a fresh wave of that sick odor hits me.

A clump of dirt falls from the dogs stomach to the floor of the patio, and I grimace.

"That one you played on my cook was particularly nasty," he tells me merrily.

A sense of wild glee flows through me, and I lean back far in the rocker, grinning widely. "You liked that one, did you?"

A bit of that unsettled prickliness dissolves, and I sigh in relief.

"Well, I didn't love the first bite of the pie, I can tell you that. Swapping salt for sugar made an impression. But when the apples turned into bugs… well, that did make me laugh."

"I wish I could have been there to see it," I say wistfully. "But I'm glad you appreciated all my effort."

"I know you Unseelie folk can't help yourself."

"The bugs were already here, you know," I tell him. "Because you keep a hovel for a home."

"And yet you're staying here with me, Purple," he says, a light in his old eyes. "What does that say about you?"

Some of my mirth disappears again, and I sigh heavily. "That my options are more limited than usual."

"And you had many options in the Underhill?" he asks mildly.

No, I start to say, but clamp my lips shut. Options are not a thing among the Unseelie. Of course, it would seem that way, that we are allowed to do as we please.

But what we are truly allowed to do, the only thing we are supposed to do, is serve at the pleasure of the Dark Queen.

I don't have an answer that I like, so I simply sit, and I rock, and I try to ignore the overpowering smell of Hash's very ugly and thus nearly charming dog.

And I try to remember what it is, exactly, that is so *off* to me about this damned inn… other than the fact it is truly in need of a deep cleaning and a serious renovation.

Or maybe a large bonfire.

"Don't even think about it," Hash says sharply.

I glance up at the old man in surprise. But no, there's no way he could know what I was thinking.

He sets the dog down, and I let out a breath as the ancient thing limps over to my chair, wagging it's pitiful tail.

And promptly leap out of it as the dog lifts a leg and begins to piss all over it.

CHAPTER SIX

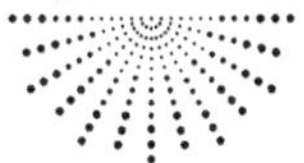

CAELAN

It takes a few days to convince the owner of Long Leaf Brews, a Star Isles clan elf with long white hair and the delicate features of her kind, to admit to me that she could use a hand.

My hands, to be exact.

Her dryad husband, a massive creature, likely from old Oak stock, watches me distrustingly as I work, inventorying the many loose-leaf tea blends they stock and making notes of what they could use more of and what might be best disposed of.

When clients come in, it's all too easy to use my innate skills and magic to divine exactly what they need.

Still, despite the pleased smiles of each client and the faultless work I've done, the male dryad doesn't trust me.

He's smart not to, and I can't say I blame him.

Unseelie fae have reputations to uphold, after all.

It's not a challenging job, not by any means, but it does come with the bonus of eavesdropping on the peaceful droning conversations of the Long Leaf Brews patrons. Hooked on caffeine, or companionship, or some blend of the above, they flock to the Star Isle elf's little café.

The trust they have in each other confounds me. Nowhere else in my life have I seen so many species sit in harmony, mingling without a care in the world.

This job, as errand boy and tea fetcher, though, it fits my purposes just fine.

They sit inside the shop with each other and speak freely, with none of the doublespeak I'm so used to. Dwarves gravitate towards a rocky corner with low-hanging ceilings and golden star-shaped lanterns, growing rowdy with every additional pot of strong black tea I bring them.

Sylphs and minotaurs sit together in another room, the former in a nearly claustrophobic green space covered in vining flowers and the latter at massive stone and pine tables lined with flickering candles.

The scent of spiced tea leaves and unlikely floral pairings permeates every conceivable nook and cranny of the place, sometimes competing with oddly opening flowers along the living walls and the scents of the customers themselves.

And yet, they do nothing to mask the smell of her, the little gold-working Wren a few blocks over.

I wake up in the small spare room we're renting in town soaked in sweat, somehow hot and cold all at once, dreams of the witch consuming me.

As a child, I heard stories of things like this: of males enchanted by witches or, worse, humans above the Underhill, of finding a mate who would never understand them. Like everyone else, I assumed they were cautionary tales.

I would never be so stupid as to find a mate match with anyone other than a fae.

Absently, I scratch at the thick tattoos around my arm and tug at my sleeve there.

A minotaur raises his hand, staring at me pointedly, the gold hoop in his nose catching the candlelight as his nostrils flare.

Right. Back to work.

I paste on my best subservient smile, which, considering the way the minotaur glares at me, must not be very convincing.

"What's it that's brought you to Wild Oak Woods?" the minotaur asks in a northern accent so thick I hardly understand him.

I pour a fresh jet of boiling water into their empty teapot, carefully doling out the specific ratio of chamomile and mint this table ordered.

The minotaur stamps a hoof impatiently, making the floorboards shake.

I give him a mild look, and when I let a bit of fang slip, he quells slightly.

"A change in my fate, I suppose," I finally answer. "Funny thing, that."

He makes a noncommittal grunt, and I glide away from the table to check on the sylphs, who titter and order more of the enchanted pastries we stock from The Pixie's Perch.

And run into Lila's hard gaze. She was brave enough to give me her name the day she hired me.

Brave, or foolish… though I'm leaning towards courage when it comes to her.

"Don't scare the minotaurs," she says, arching an eyebrow. "We don't need a stampede."

I snort. "Me, scaring them? They're twice my size."

It's not quite true, considering my fae blood gives me muscle and height, but she can't deny that they are larger than me.

She doesn't, either, instead giving me a curious, scrutinizing look that makes me feel small.

"She doesn't want you to upset anyone." Druze, her husband, a green-skinned dryad, wraps an arm around her and kisses the top of her head.

An ache goes through me, and I rub at my chest.

"Have I upset anyone?" I ask smoothly, attempting to recover. "Have there been complaints? Tell me how to improve."

I'm perturbed. Annoyance ripples along my skin.

I try to make myself small for these villagers, try to fold into myself, hide what I am, keep them comfortable and collect all the tiny clues of themselves they're only too happy to shed like breadcrumbs.

And this is how they thank me?

With coy accusations of making their patrons uncomfortable?

"I'm only too happy to hear your advice," I force out.

Lila gives me a look that tells me she's not buying any of my brand of bullshit today. I glance behind me at the minotaurs' table. Maybe she's more in the mood for their brand of it.

"Caelan," she says, flicking her long white hair over one shoulder. "Do you need the afternoon off? You seem more out of sorts —" She cuts off her words, but I hear what she was going to say.

Than usual.

More out of sorts than usual.

An Unseelie fae from the Dark Queen's court, forced to wait hand and foot on these overland peasants? A certain blonde witch haunting my sleep and my waking thoughts?

My nostrils flare.

Of *fucking* course I'm out of sorts.

"Why don't you take the afternoon off?" Lila suggests.

Druze grunts in agreement, his green eyes pinning me in place. "We are more than caught up on the work we hired you for," he adds.

I gesture around to the half-empty café. "And miss all the excitement?"

"Go. Have you even explored the town yet?" Lila makes a shooing motion with her hands. "I know it's hard to start over," she glances up at Druze, the concern around her eyes softening when she smiles at him. "It's hard," she continues. "But it can be so worth it, if you let yourself have a chance to grow."

She turns her attention back to me, and the worry and happiness on her face are what shock me the most.

Because it's real, and it's for me.

"Take a cup of lavender grey," she says, forcing a fresh tumbler into my hands. "Go walk, and see what there is to see. Come back tomorrow morning and we can talk about whatever it is that's bothering you, okay?"

I start to dip into an unctuous bow, as I might have in front of Her Dark Majesty, but pull up short because Lila might be my boss—for the moment—but she's not my queen.

I don't have a queen anymore.

I'm an Unseelie fae, out of the Underhill, and completely, utterly rudderless.

When I make myself smile back at her, I'm suddenly too tired to flash any fang, and I take the tea and her advice to get to know my new home a little better.

Starting with the witch I can't get out of my head.

CHAPTER SEVEN

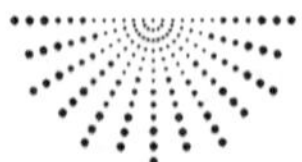

WREN

The rejection letter sits in a place of dishonor above my jeweler's bench. It mocks me, the faux-polite veneer of each sentence growing more burnished every time my gaze skates over it.

Kicked out of my coven.

Polish, polish, polish.

Rejected from the Metalsmithing Guild.

Polish, polish, polish.

Doomed to use up what little savings I have and give up completely, what with no customer base to speak of.

The metal band I've been polishing slips from my aching fingers, and I scowl up at the letter from the guild as the ring spins on the wood bench.

Fenn yips at me and I glance down at him, angry tears threatening once again.

"Maybe it is time for a break," I tell him, sniffling. "Maybe we should close up shop for the night and just go for a walk. Would you like that? Some fresh air?"

His tail flicks back and forth, but I'm not truly paying attention to him anyway.

Add bad fox-mom to my list of failures.

"What's one more?" I moan.

Fenn blinks once, unimpressed with my dramatics.

Well, that makes two of us. I push back from the bench, pulling the exquisite pair of dwarven-made loupes from my forehead.

Wincing, I stretch my arms high above my head, trying to work out the kinks and cramps in my shoulders and lower back.

I've been sitting and working for much, much too long. Lost track of time, if the darkness descending outside is any clue.

My stomach grumbles, and my mood grows blacker by the second.

What would my parents say if they could see me now?

The jewel-tone shawl my mother wove for me years ago hangs on a hook by the front door, and the knotty wood floor squeaks as I hurry over to it, wrapping it around my shoulders. My stiff fingers fumble with the key as Fenn darts out behind me and I finally manage to lock the door.

A warning rumble from Fenn sets the hair on the back on my neck standing up.

Slowly, I turn, and the reason for Fenn's upset becomes apparent immediately.

The Unseelie fae from a few days ago... was it last week? Already? I frown, rubbing my eyes and managing to scrape the key over my cheek.

"Ouch," I say, pressing my fingers to the wound.

"You've hurt yourself," he says in a low voice, stepping closer.

He's taller than I remember, and as I inhale, I catch the scent of lavender and tea.

My stomach growls, and I blink up at him owlishly, completely out of sorts.

"Have I upset you?" he asks.

"No," I tell him, frowning. Frowning harder, at least, because I'm pretty sure I've been frowning since I woke up this morning. Maybe since I fell asleep last night.

"But you are upset," he continues, taking another step towards me. "You're bleeding," he says, and before I can get together the brainpower to move, he's cupped my chin between his elegant, strong fingers. A handkerchief appears out of nowhere, and I wince as he dabs the fabric against the small cut on my cheekbone.

"Thank you," I tell him, embarrassment at how I must look starting to overpower my shock at seeing the unexpected male. "Caelan, right?"

The fae goes still, so still that it's all too clear how very different he is.

Otherworldly, from the tips of his long ears to his too sharply handsome face to his long, perfectly lean, muscled proportions.

"Did I say it wrong?" I ask, pinching the bridge of my nose. "I'm sorry. It's been a very long day, and I am out of sorts—"

"You said my name more perfectly than anyone has ever said it before," he says, the corner of his mouth quirking into a smile.

A belltower in the town center chimes three times, and I startle at the sound.

"Seven o'clock," I say. "I let time get away from me today."

My stomach makes another inelegant noise and I cringe, too tired to be afraid of this fae that I know I should be wary of.

"You're hungry," he says, a glint to his icy blue eyes.

"Yes." I pull my shawl closer around my sleeves, torn between wishing I'd put on something nicer and that I hadn't ventured out of my safe little shop at all.

"Let me take you to dinner," he says, cocking his head at me, that hint of a smile almost enough to curl my lips in response.

"Why?" I ask, looking down at myself. "I'm a mess. I have been working since daybreak, and I am afraid I would be terrible company."

"Because you said my name like it was meant for your voice." He says it so seriously that I laugh, because surely he's joking.

He tilts his head, and my laugh cuts off suddenly.

"And my boss told me to explore the town." He grins down at me, the tip of a pointed fang catching on his lower lip. "If you're not too tired, maybe I could coerce you into showing me around in exchange for a meal."

"You found work then?" Self-conscious, I tuck a piece of stray hair behind my ear, which immediately tangles in my stiff fingers. I am a mess.

Ugh.

"Mmm-hmmm," he says, the low vibration of the noise calming. I take a deep breath, coming slightly unwound, relaxing from the normalcy of simple conversation.

Huh. Who could have known all I needed was a break?

I rub my stomach. A break and some food, I decide.

"Lila at Long Leaf Brews took pity on me. She has a wonderful café, and she and her husband have been good to me." There's a hollow ring to his words, a quiet sort of questioning that echoes how I've been feeling all day. All *week*.

"I would like to get dinner with you," I tell him, deciding in that very instant.

"You would?" his smile grows sharper by the second, dangerous and alluring as all the worst ideas are.

"I would." I sigh, rubbing a hand across my face before giving him a pitiful look. "But don't say I didn't warn you. I might not be the best person to show you around Wild Oak Woods." I shrug a shoulder at the street.

The lanterns that line the street begin to glow as the sun sinks below the thatched and tiled roofs of the homes that butt up to the downtown blocks. The glass is spelled to project the light, powered by night-blooming mistflower and enchanted by Nerissa to enhance its brightness.

"It's clever spellmanship," Caelan remarks, noticing where my attention's gone. That, or mindreading is one of the many unsavory Unseelie fae attributes. "There's been a lot of thought put into this place."

He extends his elbow, and I stare at it for a beat before realizing he's offering it to me.

My cheeks flush in embarrassment, and I clumsily poke my hand through before stumbling slightly into him.

"I'm sorry," I say, my cheeks beet-red. "I'm stiff from sitting and working."

"You're not taking care of yourself," he says, a strange blue light in his eyes. "Why?"

The one word lingers in the air between us, and I turn it over as he leads me down the cobblestone street, nodding as we pass a centaur out with a pretty human woman.

"I'm worried," I finally tell him. "You don't want to hear about this," I say on the next breath.

"I wouldn't have asked if I didn't want to hear." His elbow nudges my rib cage gently, and it makes me smile.

Fenn makes careful steps next to us, glancing up at me occasionally but otherwise completely unperturbed by the fae I'm arm-in-arm with.

It's either Fenn's entirely unconcerned attitude, or a result of how absolutely wretched I've been, but I relax into him, letting him steer me around the town I've called home for a few months and have barely scratched the surface of.

It's nothing like where I'm from, the always busy and bustling eastern shore, the huge cities. Noise, smells, the sheer volume of people—getting lost in the crowd was a way of life. I thought it was perfect, the anonymity, blending in—until the coven decided my spot could be used for someone with more power, political or otherwise.

Then, cast out of the coven, my parents long dead, I was alone in a city full of creatures who didn't care to know my name.

"What was it like?" I blurt out, landing on the first question that comes into my head.

Anything to avoid those memories.

He glances sidelong at me. "The tea café?"

Thick embarrassment crawls up my throat. "No, I meant... the Underhill."

"Ah. That." He enunciates each syllable carefully. "It is not a place for those soft of heart... or hide."

I suppress a shudder. "Is that why you left?"

Quiet stretches between us. Maybe I've overstepped. Maybe that's a rude question. "I don't mean to pry—"

"I left because my friends and I were no longer welcome in the Underhill. The Dark Queen does not take lightly to those that test her authority."

I pause, glancing up at him. "You tested her authority?"

"According to her," Caelan answers shortly. "And that's all that matters."

"Why Wild Oak Woods?"

"So many questions," he says and I wince, but he lets out a soft laugh. "Because you would have us. It was the closest village and... it's amenable to us. Why are you here, then, little goldsmith?"

I blow out a breath, grimacing. "Because I got lucky. I had family leave me that shop, which I'm going to drag down with me if I can't—" I cut off abruptly, and my stomach growls again.

"I don't think you're dragging anything down at all," he muses.

"You're just being kind."

"No." A throaty, deep laugh, and another nudge of his elbow at my side. "You'll find that's not quite in my character, Wren. Here." He stops in front of a food stall, and I've been so lost in our conversation and my thoughts I hardly realized we'd made it to the heart of the downtown area.

At this time, early evening, the main square is packed with creatures and people, but they're not all buzzing to get to the next place, as they might have been in my last city.

They're lingering, the bricks underneath all manner of feet and hooves a warm, white-washed red. Rainbow buntings criss-cross overhead, food stalls stacked against each other in a riot of colorful awnings. Rich spices perfume the air, with the unmistakable scent of fried dough and grilled meat and vegetables.

A dwarven machine grates a massive block of ice under a light blue tent, a flock of winter pixies flitting around it, the bite of their cold spells tingling against my skin.

I inhale deeply, suddenly so grateful for being here that I can't stand it.

I squeeze Caelan's elbow, at a loss for words.

He smiles down at me, and it softens the sharpness of his face, just a bit.

"Thank you," I tell him, infusing the words with as much meaning as I can muster.

"Oh, no need to thank me," he says, and there's a touch of mockery to the phrase that stiffens my shoulders.

Unseelie fae, I remind myself.

Names and thanks mean different things to them than they do to us.

"Do I scare you?" he asks, and I once again wonder if he does have some kind of psychic ability to divine my thoughts.

"Scare? No, you don't scare me." I extract my hand from his elbow and pinch the bridge of my nose. "Maybe you should. Maybe I'm too tired and sad to be scared. I know I should be careful around you, and I'm not sure I have the energy right now."

Surprise lifts his eyebrows.

"Well, that won't do at all."

"What?" Thrown, I stare up at him, tilting my head. "You want me to be scared of you?"

"I have a reputation to uphold, don't I?" he drawls.

A laugh sputters out of me. "Do you?"

Caelan gestures to himself with an elegant hand. "Of course I do. Just look at me."

"Oh, yes, very intimidating," I agree, grinning widely. He's not, though, not the way he was when I first stumbled upon him in The Pixie's Perch. My initial shock at finding Unseelie fae in Wild Oak Woods has given way to... well, tired acceptance.

It's not just that, though, I suppose.

"What can I get you?" The harpy behind the counter ruffles her feathers as she waits for us, skewered meats roasting on spits on both sides of her. She casts a long look at Caelan, who seems to do his best not to notice the way she's looking at him... and the way she's sharpening her knives.

"We'll have two of each," Caelan tells her, smiling broadly, his sharp fangs on full display.

I watch him for a moment as he haggles with the harpy.

Every angle of his face is a work of art, the pointed tips of his ears begging to be touched. The way he flashes his fangs at the harpy makes me wonder what it would be like to feel them in my skin.

I shake my head and avert my eyes, certain I've been staring.

I need to start making sure I eat more. This sort of low blood sugar hazed judgment is not going to do me any favors.

And maybe make a point to get out of my own store.

And maybe I should take down that rejection letter and stop sulking.

Fenn butts his face against my ankle, and I lean down to scratch behind his ears. His tail twitches behind him and I wish, not for the first time, that I could speak outright to the familiar. I can tap his magic stores, keep him company, and get a general mood from him... but it would be nice to have a friend. A real friend, to talk to and not worry about coven politics or anything else.

By the time I stand back up, Caelan's holding several paper boats full of charred meat, steam still curling from them.

"I have some coin in my—"

"Absolutely not," Caelan interrupts. "You'll hurt my feelings if you offer to pay. This is merely in exchange for the tour you promised to give me."

The words feel formal, despite his easy smile, no fangs in sight.

"I accept." The words come out naturally, and by the way his eyes glint, I know I've said the right thing.

He tips his head towards one of the few empty stone benches in the middle of the square, and we meander through the crowd and settle in.

Fenn sits at attention as Caelan hands me the first skewer, managing to balance a trio of dipping sauces on the uneven stone bench between us.

"Bargains are usual for you, then?" I ask, picking a piece of juicy meat off the skewer and offering it to Fenn, who's only too happy to scarf it down.

"For me, or for the Unseelie, you mean?"

I pop a piece of meat into my own mouth, enjoying the burst of flavor across my tongue, and consider his question.

A quartet begins playing at the corner of the square, a lyre and a flute accompanied by a drum and a singer.

"Both, I guess," I finally answer, feeding Fenn another piece.

Caelan stares at his own meat for a moment before the entire skewer seems to disappear into his mouth.

I blink in confusion.

"Bargains are the currency of power," he answers carefully.

There hardly seemed to be enough time for him to swallow, much less chew all that meat. A tingle of uncertainty creeps across my skin, and I tug the many-colored shawl tighter around me.

"In the Queen's court, knowledge meant staying ahead of

your enemies. Bargaining for that knowledge meant staying alive, as long as you kept the upper hand."

Fascinated, I stare openly at him while I chew. "You were in the court?"

"All Unseelie fae are in her court," he says, not unkindly. "We don't have a choice."

I turn that over as I eat the rest of the skewer, braving the spiciest of the sauces to pass the time.

"That doesn't sound very nice," I manage. "It sounds terrible, actually."

"You say that, but when I bumped into you at your shop, you looked about as miserable as I felt on my worst days." He arches an eyebrow, then offers Fenn a piece of meat from one of his skewers.

Fenn's tail wags behind him as he seizes the piece of meat, making one of his funnier gurgling noises in the back of his throat.

"You know, it's odd to see a pet."

"Fenn's not a pet, not really. He's a familiar."

"All the animals in the Underhill are *her* spies."

The way he emphasizes the word makes it clear he means the fae Queen, and the pronoun drips with acid.

So, he didn't leave happily then.

I don't know why that makes me feel better. Shouldn't I feel empathy for him?

"I am an outcast too, you know."

"To outcasts." He raises his last half-eaten skewer of meat, and I laugh as we bounce the ends off each other in solidarity. "And to new beginnings."

I nod slowly, the gnawing anxiousness caused by the fact I forgot to eat most of the day slowly melting away. The night air is cool, the promise of autumn on the breeze, and the music winds through the town square along with the hum of conversation and laughter.

"Is it always like this?" he asks, raising a hand and gesturing vaguely.

"Like what?" I ask needlessly. I'm pretty sure I know what he means.

"Are they always so happy? So at peace?"

"No, of course not." I shake my head, giving the rest of the meat to Fenn, who's only too thrilled to eat the scraps. "I think everyone's just doing their best to play at it, sometimes. Happiness, I mean."

He gives me a look that makes me feel like I'm at the end of one of the sharp meat-sticks abandoned on the bench between us.

"You're unhappy," he says.

A gust of breath whooshes out from me, and I lean my hands back on the bench, tilting my chin up and inspecting the purpling sky overhead. The stone's rough against my palms.

"I shouldn't be." That's the truth of it. "I have everything I need to be happy. A beautiful home, a shop I was lucky enough to inherit with a full inventory, wonderful new friends, and then of course, there is Fenn," I say, and my sweet familiar bounds into my lap, whuffling at my chin before circling and settling in.

I curl over him, running my hands over his soft fur, loving the musky scent of him and the adorable way his white whiskers twitch.

"But something is missing," Caelan urges.

A hint of smoke spills into the air, the crackling of magic. I go still, turning my attention slowly to him.

He's watching me carefully, those ice-blue eyes taking my measure.

"I'm not interested in a bargain," I tell him, making myself laugh.

"I wasn't offering one," he says, frowning. "That's your magic, not mine."

"It wasn't mine," I insist, pushing at his shoulder in annoyance.

He lets out a laugh. Without warning, he seizes my wrist and brushes the barest of kisses on top of my hand.

My heart stutters. I stare up at him, wide-eyed and suddenly, too late, terrified.

Terrified, and *alive*.

"It was yours, little gold witch, and you should be smarter than to walk around offering up pieces of yourself with ears like mine listening." There's a bite to his words, a cruelty that makes me sit up straighter.

"I don't see anything wrong with your ears." I return my attention to Fenn, annoyed at both myself and the way my cheeks heat, and at the fae for making me feel heard.

For making me want to tell him my problems, consequences be damned.

"I think your ears are beautiful, just like the rest of you," I finish, feeling bold and ridiculous all at once.

A rough laugh skates from his lips, and I stand up abruptly, pulling Fenn to my chest before depositing him back on the white-washed bricks.

"I say we get some spiced cider and, ah," I squint, looking for the tell-tale green and navy checked awning, "some of the chocolate basil twists." I'm not sure entirely what's gotten a hold of me tonight but for once, for once, I'm out of my head.

I'm out of my head and I'm not thinking about the goddess-damned guild or my coven, and maybe that's enough for me to enjoy myself.

A smile spreads across my face, and I turn back to look at Caelan, gesturing for him to come with me.

His answering smile is bright, and his eyes dance with merriment.

I like when he looks at me like that, I decide.

I'd like for him to look at me like that more often.

CHAPTER EIGHT

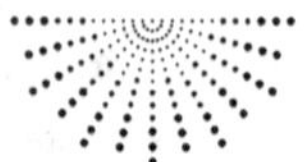

CAELAN

The golden witch hands me a twisted bit of fried black dough, the sweet scent of basil tingling my nostrils and the hot grease soaking through the parchment paper wrapper.

I sniff at it, taking a cautious bite.

"Unghf," I tell her, my eyes wide in surprise.

"So good, isn't it?" She takes a bite of her own, dropping a few coins back into the pocket of her dress and tugging me along to the next stall, where a deep red cherry cider simmers on a cauldron over a birch bark fire.

A few more coins exchange hands while I inhale the chocolate dough, a delightful mix of bitter and sweet and herbal flavors, and then Wren's pressing a striped paper cup full of steaming cherry cider into my hand.

"It's got a bit of a bite to it," she warns, then polishes off her dough twist before sipping at her own cider. "It's strong," she says with a cough.

The vendor, a centaur with a deep chestnut hide and an

overly friendly smile, chuckles. "Sorry, about that. This one fermented at a different level."

"It's delicious," she says, and his grin turns slightly predatory as she takes another drink.

"Do you live around here, then?" the centaur asks, his red-brown tail flicking behind him.

"We do," I answer for her, wrapping my arm around her waist and pulling her close.

She stiffens slightly at my touch, but the centaur just raises an eyebrow, some of his smile disappearing.

Good.

"Thank you so much," I tell him, and he steps back a bit when my fangs appear.

As for Wren, she sips her spiked cider with raised eyebrows. Sighing, I detach my arm from her waist and offer her my elbow again.

Unfortunately, now that I know what she feels like in my arms, I fear my dreams will be even more vivid.

"What was that about?" she asks, her lovely lips pursed.

"I didn't like how he was leering at you."

"He wasn't leering," she says with a laugh.

"He was, and he would have followed you home if you said you had a carrot for him," I continue. "Not even a sugar cube. A lowly carrot, and he would have been eating out of your hand. Though I'm sure he was much more interested in eating what's between your legs."

"*Caelan*," she whispers my name in a completely scandalized tone, and I rake my hand through my hair in annoyance at myself.

I don't want her sounding like that when she whispers my name. I want her to sound like she's unraveling, coming undone, with my mouth and only my mouth between her legs, feasting on her.

Fuck.

Is this what I've become? From one of the highest courtiers of the Dark Queen to a dissolute elf topside, craving the taste of a mortal witch?

How the mighty have fallen.

I glance over at her, though, and there's no denying my growing attraction to her. Her cheeks are bright pink, whether from my tasteless comment or the chill in the air, I'm not sure, but I want to run the pads of my fingers across her skin and test their warmth.

I want to lick at the chocolate crumb stuck to her lower lip, to see what the spiced cherry cider tastes like on her tongue, and the foolish, stupid piece of me that guesses what she could be would risk it all for that chance.

A witch. A *fucking* witch.

"Don't look at me like that," she says, patting at her snarled hair. Snarled, and in desperate need of a comb.

"*Why* are you sad?" I ask her, surprising us both with the question.

"Why are you sad?" she repeats, glaring at me.

I snort a laugh, and she half-smiles.

"You said you were an outcast too," I press, looking for an advantage. It wouldn't do to become entangled long-term with a witch, of course… but maybe I can whet my appetite for her in other ways.

I nearly nod to myself, but catch the movement at the last minute.

"Is that why you're sad?" I ask.

"Do fae usually ask such blunt questions?"

"Do witches usually avoid them?" I counter.

She comes to a standstill in front of a strange little building. Deep blue plaster flakes in several places, and a small sign simply boasts an etching of stars.

I sniff in disdain.

"I was rejected from a business organization I would like to be a part of."

My mouth drops open in surprise. "Your work is exquisite."

It's not a lie, either. The few moments I took this evening watching her work, studying the pieces on display in the window, proved her to be nothing short of a master of her craft, possessing both goldsmith and lapidary skills at a level I didn't know mortals were even capable of.

"Oh," she says, her eyes widening, a fresh wave of rosy pink washing across her cheeks. "You don't have to say that."

"It's true," I tell her. I need her to know that—it's the least she deserves.

"This is Nerissa's home," she says, turning away, pleased and embarrassed at my praise.

I like the way she looks right now.

I'll have to lavish kind words upon her.

I wonder if she's that susceptible to praise in bed, as well.

"Nerissa," I repeat, my annoyance at the centaur dissolving at the idea of her coming around my cock while I tell her what a good job she's doing.

"She is a spellsmith," Wren tells me. "Best I've ever met, and in the city—" Her voice breaks, and she looks down at her shoes.

A bit threadbare for my tastes. I should find her something more suitable.

"In the city that cast you out?" I guess, mining for information the same way a dwarf would sniff out a vein of precious ore.

"Not the city, so much." A lopsided grin curves up half her mouth. "The coven I was in, however, they did the casting out. And now the guild I need on my side to find clients, you know, their shining endorsement on my door so people don't think their wrists and fingers are going to turn green or worse, that their dicks are going to shrivel and fall off."

"Shrivel and fall off?" I repeat, pulling a pained face. "Why would you make someone's dick shrivel and fall off? Is that the type of spellwork you're doing on those things?"

She barks a laugh, the humor shining on her face and transforming her from merely pretty to the stunning creature I saw when she first breezed into my life.

There's no chance my cock's going to be anything but hard when she's around.

And now she's offered up exactly what it is she wants: the guild, delivered to her on a silver platter. A coven of sister witches.

Wren the golden witch wants a home, and she wants a business, and I'm liable to do just about whatever it takes to make all her wishes come true.

For a price.

CHAPTER NINE

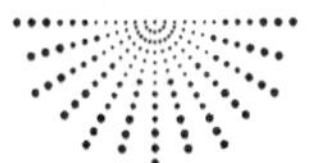

WREN

By the time Caelan walks me back home, I've pointed out my friends' homes and storefronts, some of the shops I like best, and some I haven't wandered into yet, and I managed to extract a promise that he won't do anything untoward with the information I've offered up.

The bargain I struck was easy enough to make, considering this has been the easiest evening I've spent since moving to Wild Oak Woods, the hours slipping by with laughter and Caelan's quick wit.

He's not like anyone I've ever met before, not at all, from the way he's curious and wide-eyed about nearly everything we come across to the way he seems highly put upon, reminding me of a noblewoman I once had the misfortune of working on a custom piece for when I was first starting out, years ago.

Now, we stand back in the warm, familiar glow of Witch-work's Jewelry, Fenn long since disappeared into the woods to hunt or do whatever it is that fox familiars do when off-duty.

"This was really… nice," I say, fishing in my pocket for the heavy iron key that will unlock the door.

"Nice?" he asks, a hint of a sardonic smile on his lips. "Consider me damned by faint praise."

"You are so ridiculous," I say, huffing a laugh and shaking my head in disbelief. I grin up at him, pleased but slightly confused by the budding pleasure deep in my chest. He's not just beautiful, but charming, and clever, with a streak of self-confidence paired with self-effacing humor that resonates with me.

I didn't know I had a type when it comes to men—frankly, I've always been too busy and concerned with… literally everything else about surviving day-to-day to even consider men as more than a passing way to scratch an itch.

A very particular itch, one I haven't even thought about since moving to Wild Oak Woods.

Now, though, with Caelan's sharp, otherworldly features, whimsical speech and debonair flair… I'm thinking about it.

That's the thing about an itch—once you've thought of it, there's nothing more aggravating than not being able to scratch it.

His nostrils flare, and he take a step closer to me. "Just nice, then, little witch? That's all this was… was *nice*?" The word drips with derision, but instead of being annoying, it's hilarious.

"Don't get in a snit about it," I tell him, arching an eyebrow. "It's not your fault that my standards are so high. You'll just have to try harder to meet them."

He takes another step, and suddenly, I'm backed up against the heavy oak door, the lion-shaped door knocker digging into my shoulder.

One of his large, lavender hands splays against the door by my head, the other near my waist, not quite touching me.

My breathing grows quick.

Caelan's caged me in, caught me like a mouse in a trap, his

light blue eyes dilating as his breath warms the cold tip of my nose.

My eyes drop to his mouth, and I lick my lips.

Is he going to kiss me? Do I want him to kiss me? What if my breath is bad after the greasy street food? What if I'm being stupid by wanting to be kissed by an Unseelie fae?

My gaze darts back to his eyes, my breath hitching slightly as his head dips lower.

I stretch up on my tiptoes, reaching for him, wanting to close the distance between us, wanting to find out how bad of an idea this is—

When he straightens, there's a hint of a smile on his lips.

"Goodnight, little Wren. Thank you for a lovely evening. Sweet dreams."

With that, he disappears into the gloaming dark, leaving me reeling and open-mouthed against the door to my shop, all alone.

It takes me far longer than I'd like to admit to recover fully.

Shock turns into shame, shame into indignation, and indignation into annoyance.

Why would he make me think he was going to kiss me?

Why wouldn't he just kiss me?

I hold my palm up to my lips, huffing out and testing my breath. I wince. It is, in fact, a bit strange-smelling.

"It's for the best," I mutter to myself, jamming my key into the lock and turning it until it gives a satisfying opening click.

Still, my heart's beating too fast. My skin's oversensitive, and I shudder as I unwrap the woven shawl from my shoulders.

A whispered word lights a lantern—a simple spell, one of the few I use outside of my jewelry work—and I pick up the enchanted silver and glass light and begin to head to the stairs at the back of the shop when a sight brings me up completely short.

The sight of me in the mirror.

My stomach drops, and I cringe at my reflection.

My hair, which I haven't bothered with lately, looks like a

fucking scarecrow. Bits of yellow-blonde hair stick out in messy tufts; the braid I thought I'd neatly done this morning looks to be several days old, not a matter of daylight hours.

There are dark purple circles under my eyes, a brown smattering of leftover summer freckles standing out garishly on pale skin. Even my eyes are less blue than usual, more stormy grey and so, so tired-looking.

No wonder he didn't want to kiss me.

There's a stain on my dress too, and I stare at it in growing horror.

Caelan was the very picture of elegance and style, and meanwhile, I look like I've been sleeping at my jeweler's bench for the last month straight.

Gross.

Scowling, I stamp upstairs, determined to do better.

"I didn't start over here just to let myself turn into a bog witch," I mutter, my feet falling heavy and satisfying on the wood treads.

I unlock the second door to my apartment, probably unnecessary here in Wild Oak Woods, but a habit from living in the less than idyllic city that I doubt I'll drop anytime soon.

If ever.

Breathing deeply, I lock the door behind me, taking off my threadbare shoes and gathering myself.

In the city, I wanted to blend in. I didn't want to stand out, I didn't want to be an easy target for the many nefarious characters who were only too ready to pounce on anyone they deemed worthy of their attention.

Especially after my parents passed—it was enough to simply carry on waking up and working every day.

Being clean was enough. Being presentable was hardly my top priority in those days, especially early on after their deaths, when I could hardly move for grief.

Fenn was the sole reason I was able to feed myself most days, and then, when the attorney came to tell me this shop had been deeded to me, in this tiny hamlet so far outside anywhere I'd ever lived, suddenly, things seemed possible again.

I would have an actual storefront, not just the hand-me-down clients of my parents looking for renewed spells on worn-out charms and trinkets.

I could hone my skills far away from the thundering noise of the city.

I could finally earn my way into the guild.

Then the coven kicked me out, because without my parents, what was I?

A nobody.

I blow out a breath, trying to blow out all that negativity with it.

Maybe it's time to try harder. Maybe it's time to be so good that the damned guild can't ignore me.

And maybe, just maybe, it's time to do something about the covenless crew of witches who decided to make me their friend.

Maybe it's time to be more than just Wren who owns Witchwork's Jewelry.

It's time to be worthy of that responsibility.

I brew a cup of herbal tea, slowly, methodically, a ritual that's earned its place in every nighttime wind-down, and I pull out a piece of parchment from a long-forgotten desk drawer.

My ink pot's nearly dried up, and I frown as I jab my freshly sharpened quill into it, finally giving in and dropping in some hot water.

Finally, I scratch out a few words on the paper, hoping it will settle the turbulence within me.

I read the words back out loud, hearing an echo of my mother's cadence, imagining the brush of her hand against my cheek when I was a young girl determined to prove myself with the rest of the fledgling witches.

Be so good they can't ignore you.

I miss her. I miss them both.

It's time to take her advice to heart and be the witch she raised me to be.

I tuck the parchment under my pillow before I get dressed for bed, and when I finally lie down on it, I can almost imagine I hear her words in my ears.

CHAPTER TEN

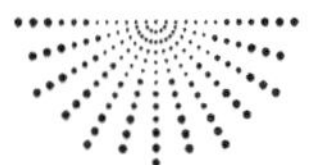

WREN

An unfamiliar rustling wakes me just after dawn. The first rosy fingers of light drift across the pale butterscotch-yellow quilt, and I jerk upright, tucking it around me.

Fenn's curled up in a red fluffy donut beside my feet, one eye sleepily peeking out from behind his bristle brush tail.

My heart leaps into my throat, and my hands fist the soft linen.

The rustling noise stops, and Fenn sits up, his amber eyes finding mine.

"Go," I hiss at him.

He jumps off the bed on velvet paws, not one chittering yap or yowl to be heard.

His silence doesn't make me feel better.

A split second later, a crash sounds from the main part of my apartment and I bolt out of bed, unwilling to let Fenn take the brunt of whatever assault is happening.

"That's my fox," I yelp, brandishing the first thing I land on, which happens to be my silver and glass lantern.

There's no one there.

The main rooms are empty, the little postage stamp of a kitchen neat and sparkling, the teacup I left out the night before put away.

My jaw drops.

There's not a speck of dust to be found, anywhere, at all.

"My shoes," I say on a gasp, the silver lantern dropping from my hand to the thick rug on the floor with a thud.

My slippers, which I admit have been in desperate need of replacing, are no longer in a state of depressing disrepair.

The cracked, sad leather shines bright from a fresh oiling, and the plain beige they were last night has been replaced by a deep emerald green.

I frown at them in confusion.

Fenn yips, pointing his nose at the corner nearest the door to the stairs.

A high-pitched chittering sounds from the area he's fixated on, and my brain finally clicks the pieces into place.

"A brownie?" I whisper, shocked into speaking out loud. "I thought they were extinct."

The chittering grows more agitated, and I snap my mouth shut and spring into action, scrambling over to the kitchen.

"Fenn, leave the poor thing alone." Fenn growl-yips at me, but listens, settling for following me around. It takes me a moment to find my favorite floral bone china teacup, the gilded lip worn but still pretty and serviceable.

The milk I brought home from the grocer a few days ago still smells fresh enough in the cold box where I keep it and a few other foodstuffs, enchanted to keep everything at a safe temperature by the same ice pixies who make the snow in the town square.

I fill the milk up to the top of the fragile teacup, uncork the tall copper canister half-full of sugar cubes and fish one out for good measure, plunking it into the milk with a shrug.

"I'm not entirely sure what you like, friend, but I can't thank you enough for your help." The words are hushed and measured, and I'm doing my very best not to completely freak out.

A brownie! In my house.

I clear my throat, not sure if it's rude to look at the tiny creature, or if I'm risking scaring it away for good by trying to sneak a peek, and set the delicate antique cup on the table.

"I can leave it for you at night, if you prefer. I appreciate your help around here, and I'm glad to make your acquaintance." It sounds oddly formal, a total contrast to my bare feet, cold on the colorful rug, and my too-short, thin white shift.

And the fact I'm pretty sure my hair still looks like shit.

"Okay, uh, I'm going to go get ready for the day."

Fenn sniffs, his whiskers twitching, giving me a look that tells me plain as day just how little he thinks of me talking to any magical creature other than him.

"I left you a boar bristle brush and a comb on your vanity," a tiny voice like the tinkling of bells says in my ear. "The fae have taken an interest in you, witchling. It wouldn't do to look less than presentable."

"Oh." I grasp around for how to answer that. The fae? *The* fae? Does the brownie mean Caelan?

I frown, not sure if I like the idea of him sending this creature over here, or if I'm offended by the fact he spent a few hours in my company last night and decided I needed magical intervention.

It hurts my feelings that he might have been right about that.

"That was kind of you," I say awkwardly. "Let me know if you prefer something else to eat."

I smooth my hands down the creased fabric of my shift, feeling out of my depth.

"The Seelie Queen told me of a baker witch blessed with the

perfect scone recipe," the brownie says. Something tickles against my ear, and I stand very still.

The Seelie Queen. So not Caelan, then. A completely, entirely different fae is interested in me.

I'm even less sure what to do with that information.

Fenn's nose twitches even faster.

Piper's the only baker witch in town, and I'm glad I can at least remember that fact after the brownie casually name dropped the Seelie Queen like it's nothing.

"Would you like me to bring you scones tonight? From next door?" I venture.

The tinkling sound grows brighter, faster, and a strangely heavy pressure settles on my shoulder.

Fenn makes a sound low in his throat, and I very, very slowly look at the creature now perched on my person.

"I would like the blueberry scones with the spiced walnuts and the cheeriness spell," the brownie says, the words so high and fast I have to strain to make them out.

It's furry—no, fuzzy, really, a light, silken fuzz coating every inch of the little faerie's body. Golden wings twinkle in the early light, inordinately long fingers tipped in claws at its sides. Vertically elongated pupils, like a cat, blink at me beneath a lush fringe of eyelashes.

"Cheeriness spell," I repeat, slightly dizzy.

"That would be nice," the brownie says, dipping her head in agreement. "Your offer is accepted."

The tiny thing levitates from my shoulder, appearing on the table in the blink of an eye and lapping at the cup of milk and sugar like a cat. I study it for a moment, boggled and out of sorts, noting the finely furred ears on the top of its head.

Strange.

"I'll just… leave you to it," I say.

Slowly, because I don't want to upset the thing, I retreat to my bedroom and shut the door behind me, nearly closing Fenn out.

"A brownie?" I murmur, and Fenn's huge ears perk up.

A brownie. Who wants blueberry scones with spiced walnuts and a cheeriness spell, who left me brushes and cleaned my house and mended my shoes. More than mended my shoes, really.

Those emerald slippers are *so* much better than new.

The brownie must have tended to my room last night too, because now that I'm not sitting stock still in bed, terrified, it's easy to see that everything's been given a shine, dusted to perfection, and the small worn-out spots in my bedding have been carefully patched.

"Wow," I manage.

The boar bristle brush and comb the brownie told me about do, in fact, sit on the vanity, and they're much, much nicer than any set I've ever owned.

The Seelie Queen sent the brownie?

My nose crinkles as I mull it over, but my brain doesn't present any answer or explanation or, sadly, any outlandish theories, either.

It's a good sign, though… isn't it?

Anxiety tightens my chest, and I rub the heel of my hand over it. Maybe I'll get myself a blueberry scone with spiced walnuts and a cheeriness charm too.

My gaze lands on the brush set again.

Or maybe all I need is to take care of myself—brush my hair and clean myself up and put my best foot forward, and be so damned good that the guild can't ignore me.

I nod and sit at the tiny vanity and begin the tedious work of unsnarling my hair before I make good on my promise to myself.

THE CHILL from the evening hasn't quite dissipated as I finally open the door to my shop, double-checking to ensure it locks behind me. Fenn's tucked by the hearth again, napping away the morning as he always does, but for once, I'm not napping with him.

Mist clings to the cobblestone streets, the few early risers up and about at this hour moving quickly to their destinations.

My heart's a hummingbird in my chest, buzzing with something between excitement and anxiety.

At least I have the comfort of knowing I've done my best to make myself presentable.

I close my eyes, inhaling deeply through my nostrils to calm myself and take the first steps from my doorway.

The leather satchel digs into my shoulder and I readjust it as I walk, passing by the already busy Pixie's Perch. If I go there first, I might lose my nerve, and I'm still determined to do this… for now, at least.

I'll save the familiar pastels and Piper's friendship as a reward for pushing myself from my comfort zone. And I'll get two blueberry cheeriness scones to go.

A golden glint catches my eye as I walk past the darkened window of another store, and it takes me a half-second to realize it's my reflection—my hair now neatly managed into cascading waves down one shoulder.

I stand a little straighter, pleased with the results of my work, and carry on down the street towards my first destination.

A little kernel of irritation tries to sprout as I stand outside the huge corner storefront because I've managed to avoid going here the entirety of the few months I've lived in Wild Oak Woods, telling myself I needed to at least achieve something before I rewarded myself with a visit to what's sure to be one of my favorite places in the whole village.

The bookstore.

Not just any bookstore, either, but a massive, luxurious space. Dwarven-made ladders

Warm light glows from the windows, proving the witch owner I've met in passing is already beginning her day.

"You can do this," I mutter to myself, and with that, I clutch the door handle and pull it open.

Much too hard because it swings open easily, and I stumble for a second, completely off-balance.

"Oh," the witch who owns the store startles, peering at me from behind thick round spectacles, her hair neatly braided in a crown around her head. "Good morning, are you alright?"

"Sorry, it wasn't as heavy as I expected." A small laugh bubbles out of me, and the witch smiles.

"Wren, right? From down the street? The jeweler?" She squints at me, stepping off the ladder.

"That's right, hi, and you're Ruby? Sorry I haven't stopped by before now, I should have. This place is amazing."

It's completely true.

A fire crackles somewhere deep in the shop, and I peer around for a second, enchanted by the entire store. The distinctive smell of paper and ink, along with something floral and woodsy, permeates the air. A cat naps on one of the many little tables, perfect for curling up with a book or for quiet conversation with a friend.

"You've been settling in, no need to apologize. Is there something you're looking for today?"

"You, actually," I blurt out, then cringe slightly as she blinks owlishly at me. "What I mean to say is, I am, ah, attempting to do a better job at getting out of my store and getting around town." I gesture vaguely at the gorgeously styled shelves, the gilded leather-bound books and the glass stands housing parchment paper and ink and all manner of stationery.

"And I was first on your list?" She beams at me. "I'm honored. And I'm sorry to say I understand exactly what you mean. It's hard to get away from work when you live with it, isn't it?"

"Do something you love and you'll never work a day in your life, you'll work every day all day and never be satisfied with how much you've done." I cock my head, pleased when she laughs again. "I don't think that's how the saying goes—"

"But it should," Ruby exclaims, clapping her hands together. "Here, what do you like to read? I can put together a list for you, that's the least I can do."

I hadn't thought that far ahead, and suddenly, I can't think of one damned thing I've read for fun. Ever. I'm not sure I even know how to read now.

"Do you have any books on local lore, or, uh, maybe on local geology?"

"Sure, of course—we actually had a rush for a certain gemstone years and years ago…" She trails off, disappearing behind another shelf.

I pick my way around it carefully, not wanting to upset anything in the store, still weighed down with my bag.

"I also like romances," I offer, finally remembering a fact about myself.

"Oh, me too. We have a romance book club that meets monthly, every third Wednesday, if you want to come. I've been trying to get Piper to come for ages but she always says she has to wake up early and bake."

Ruby reappears, holding a couple of books in her arms. "Here. The next books on our club list aaaaand a short history of local caves. I think it covers Wild Oaks geology, but if it's not what you had in mind, come back and we'll find another option."

"I have something for you too," I say, feeling slightly shy and overwhelmed, but determined to finish what I came here for.

"You do?" Ruby pats her braids, setting the books on what must be her check-out counter. "You didn't have to do that."

"Well, I didn't, of course not, but I'm not just doing it out of pure selflessness." I cringe. That sounds so much worse than I meant.

"What I mean is, I don't get a lot of walk-in clientele at my store, so I thought I would take some of my creations and loan them out. You don't have to take it, I don't have any expectation of payment, just that you'd tell anyone who asks where you got it."

I'm too afraid to look back at her, instead rummaging around in my leather satchel for the earrings I picked out for her. "These are opal and rose gold studs, enchanted to assist with focus. They need to recharge monthly in the full moon, but should help when you need to concentrate." The words tumble out in a river over each other, and when I finally locate the earrings, I triumphantly put the little suede box on her counter.

Ruby's staring at me, open-mouthed. "This is quite a gift."

I shrug. "They were just sitting in my shop. I'd rather they be put to use. How much do I owe you for the books?"

"Stop it. You're not paying me for the damned books." She laughs, opening up the suede box, then sighing as she runs her fingertips over them. "Beautiful. And there's no catch?"

"No, not at all." My mouth twists to the side. "Is this too strange? Me bringing these? You don't have to take them—" I reach out for the box.

She swats at my hand. "Absolutely not. You've loaned them to me, and now I've seen them and I'm attached. And if you don't show up for book club, I'm going to be mad. Bring Piper and tell her to bring petit fours."

"It's a deal," I tell her.

The opals glint in the morning light, and she clucks her tongue in appreciation before fastening them to her ears.

"Well, consider me your new friend," Ruby declares. "Book club, third Wednesday, and I'll drag you from your store if you don't show up." She looks me up and down. "Are you going to the other shops with loans like this?"

"That was my plan." I shrug a shoulder, trying to squash the lingering self-doubt.

"You're not worried about being taken advantage of? Or someone selling them out from under you?"

"Of course I am." I bite my lip. "But I don't know how else to drum up business."

"Your coven isn't sending you clients?" There's a strange undercurrent to the question, and I glance sidelong at her.

"Is your coven? Sending you clients?"

"I'm not in one." Ruby sighs, and her cat jumps on the desk. It's a long-haired calico, with a fluffy tail even Fenn might envy. "Most of us aren't, I think. Covenless witches and creatures, that's Wild Oak Woods."

"Hmm." I'm not quite ready to dive into another coven, and I'm definitely not ready to head up all the work that comes with starting one... but it's odd. It's odd that the witches here are all without a coven.

"Have you ever seen a brownie?" I ask, the question tumbling out before I've thought better of it.

Her brow furrows, and her eyes go distant. "No, I don't think so. They're going extinct, like all the Seelie fae, aren't they?"

"I thought so too."

Ruby purses her mouth, wrapping up the books she's selected in a thick, brown waxy paper. Red and white twine follows, and she slips a couple pretty bookmarks into the package with quick, efficient movements.

"You've seen a brownie, then." It's not a question.

"You don't seem surprised."

She presses her palms against the counter, the familiar flutter of a witch's power emanating from her.

"Things are... different lately, right? Lots of changes. The Unseelie fae in town, a brownie now, and a village full of witches without coven."

We share a look, but neither of us say anything else for a long moment.

A log pops in the fire, and she pushes the wrapped books towards me.

"Maybe we should have a different kind of book club soon. Just in case."

"A different kind of book club," I echo. "What do you have in mind?"

She shakes her head. "I don't know yet, but when I do, I'll be sure you're with us."

I tuck the waxy package into my satchel, pulling the little jewelry boxes I've made on top. "Thank you," I say, smiling at her. "I'm glad I finally came in."

"Me too. Don't be a stranger, or I'll be forced to come visit you when you're rolling out of bed or all set to read a book with a cup of tea."

I snort. "I love a little light threatening in the morning." I give a slight wave, headed for the door and to my next stop.

"Go under her light," Ruby calls out as I leave, the common witch phrase settling something deep and restless in my soul.

I might still be new in Wild Oak Woods, but I've never been alone.

CHAPTER ELEVEN

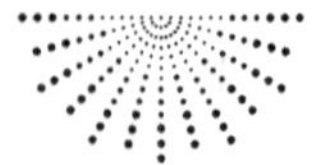

CAELAN

*D*warves. So many dwarves.

They've taken over the entire front room of Long Leaf Brews, ordering the strongest black tea by the pot, and it's a damned good thing I inventoried it earlier this week because I know exactly how much we have to sell.

Lila and Druze flit amongst the tables, looking like giants in the crowd.

The entire café is abuzz with them.

With dwarves, and with the rumor of why they're here.

"Dragon sapphire," the table nearest me roars, slamming their mugs on the table. "May we find it, may we mine it, and may we grow rich and fat."

The dwarves all roar their approval.

I raise an eyebrow.

So far, it seems all they're going to do is drink all the black tea we have, but who am I to judge?

I'm uniquely qualified to judge, actually, and it's one of my favorite pastimes, but at least these dwarves have a goal.

Meanwhile, I'm just serving tea and picking up gossip.

"What is dragon sapphire?" Lila asks Druze quietly.

Not quietly enough, because the entire room goes silent as soon as she utters the question.

"What is dragon sapphire?!" a rowdy dwarf yells. His bright orange hair is braided into his grey-spattered beard. The dwarves erupt into raucous exclamations of disbelief.

Druze sighs heavily, and Lila's cheeks indent as she bites them.

Smirking, I drop off another fresh-brewed pot of tea at the ginger dwarf's table, half-listening and half-daydreaming of Wren again.

Wren, who haunts my dreams and my waking thoughts, the little witch's scent tickling my nose even more after spending time with her last night.

Wren of the quiet laughter and clever words, with strange tastes in food and stranger tastes in hair styles… or lack thereof.

I'm not sure if I'm worse off for spending time with her or happier now that I have.

Ga'Rek and Kieran were both asleep by the time I returned to our rented rooms, Ga'Rek snoring so loud that it's a wonder the prince was able to sleep at all.

"Dragon sapphire is only the best stone to hold enchantments, though the witch or wizard who tries to do so must be talented beyond compare."

"Dead tricky to work with," another dwarf chimes in, hefting his axe.

Druze puts a green hand on the top of the ax and flatly pushes it down. The dwarf blushes crimson as he stows it away in its sheath on his back.

"For enchantments," I repeat, delight ricocheting through me like a stone skipped on a lake. "This stone is used for enchanting? This one, the dragon sapphire you say you've found near here?"

"Aye!" the dwarves chorus, mugs and palms slapping the tables at once.

Lila quirks an eyebrow at me, my sudden interest piquing her own.

"And it's rare," I press. "And only the best mages can use it?"

"That's what we said, lad, are you dense?"

"Very dense," I tell the dwarf, topping off his mug with scalding-hot tea. "Very dense and very interested in all things that have to do with this ore."

"Oho, boyo here thinks he can beat us to the dragon sapphire," another dwarf cries, and Lila winces as they all begin shouting and clamoring once again.

"I didn't say that."

"You're an Unseelie, you don't have to say shit. We all know shit's coming out of your mouth one way or another." The dwarves laugh uproariously, and I feel the tips of my ears go hot, my rage slithering like a snake from under a rock into the daylight.

My fangs bite into my lower lip as I smile, growing sharper in my mouth, longer the angrier I get.

"Enough," Lila yells. "If you insult my friend, you'll find yourself without tea."

That gets their attention—and mine, too.

The pressure of my lengthening fangs lessens, and I swivel my gaze up to the white-haired elf, who stands with her hands on her hips, her nose pink with fury.

Druze blinks slowly at me, then nods at his wife's words. "You treat him with respect, just as he's done to you." He glowers at the dwarves, who manage to become very interested in their steaming black tea, then begin mumbling apologies.

"Oy, there, lad," says the ginger dwarf. "They didn't mean any harm. Can't say my people have gotten along with your lot in the past, but anyone who's interested in the lore of the ore is alright in my book."

I refrain from calling him an idiot out of respect for Lila and Druze, and I also refrain from inspecting too closely the surge of warmth I feel towards the couple.

They're only my employers, after all, they're not truly friends. Displeasure curls through me.

My current obsession with the mortal witch is enough trouble without inviting full-fledged friendship with a Star Isles elf and a dryad into my life.

"No harm done?" the dwarf asks, his bushy eyebrows twitching. There's a trace of fear in his brown eyes.

Delicious. They should be afraid of me.

The Unseelie fae are not to be trifled with. We are a proud species with a proclivity for vengeance and an excellent ability to hold petty grudges.

Even the ones cast out from the Underhill.

"No harm at all," I make myself say, memorizing his face, just in case. "By the way, I know a witch of superb caliber who would no doubt bring justice to your dragon sapphires."

With that, I stalk off to the back of the shop.

Only a week or so since I left the Underhill, and already I've gotten softer.

I should blame the witch, no doubt it lies with the lovely Wren's undue influence over me, even though she's unaware of it.

But I do wonder if maybe the fault, this growing softness, is only of my own making.

I will have to remedy it.

My fangs fully extend and I pace around the back room, rummaging for more of the absurdly strong black tea the dwarves are quickly running through.

May they all have acute kidney failure.

"Hey," Lila's voice coasts across the room, and I look up to see the Star Isles elf standing on the threshold, concern clear in her eyes.

She's too kind for her own good. They all are, these topsiders, too kind and trusting.

Easy pickings.

Easy pickings.

Of course. Of fucking course. I shouldn't be looking to romance the little witch, to have my way with her after patience and boring courtship.

No, trapping her would be so, so much more satisfying. And then I could scratch the ridiculous itch I have for the mortal and be rid of her, no lasting harm done.

I smile at Lila, and she flinches.

"Are you alright?" she asks, mustering the question despite her misgivings towards me, clear on her face. "If you need to take the afternoon to clear your head, or if you want to work back here—"

"I will take the day," I tell her. "With pay." I make sure to sneer at her for good measure.

She stands straighter. "Good. I'm proud of you for putting yourself first. You can't take care of anyone else if you don't take care of yourself."

My jaw drops at her impudence. As if I have ever put anyone before me?

How absurd.

Still, I can't think of a comeback before she smiles softly again, leaving me with a room full of tea for company.

A room full of tea, and the beginnings of a plan to trap my witch, something I'm *certain* will put me in a much better mood.

The dwarves might be idiots, but at least they've given me *something* to work with.

CHAPTER TWELVE

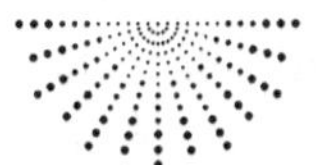

The first dwarf who comes into my shop is positively vibrating with energy as he looks around.

I'm completely drained from my early morning of small talk and extroversion, and despite feeling hopeful my efforts will pay off, I can't help but be miffed by a potential customer's appearance all the same.

His hands tremble as he fingers a gold pendant on display, and I inwardly sigh and put away the ruby-studded ring I've been polishing.

"Hello, how can I help you today?"

"You're the witch who cast the enchantment on this?" he asks gruffly. The axe on his back is nicked and dented from use, his beard hanging nearly to his knees. His brown eyes are hardly visible beneath the amount of facial hair on him.

"Yes, I enchanted all the items you see here. Are you in the market for a secret keeper charm, then?" I nod at the pendant in his hands.

"I heard tell of a witch whose work was worthy of a dragon sapphire," he says by way of answering.

I stop in my tracks. "Dragon sapphire?"

"Ah, I see you've heard of it." He nods, clearly happy with my response.

"Dragon sapphire," I repeat. "Is that why you're here, in Wild Oak Woods? There's a vein of them around here?"

My hands twitch, and before he can answer, I whip back around to the main counter, where I've stowed my leather satchel.

"Book, book, where is the book," I murmur, pulling out the wax-paper-wrapped set Ruby sent me on my way with.

"Are you up to the challenge of enchanting a dragon sapphire?" the dwarf asks. "Your metalsmithing is… somewhat lacking, but your stone cutting is acceptable and that secret keeper charm seems strong enough."

I sputter. "Somewhat lacking?"

"Aye, but we're not all blessed with dwarven skill."

I scowl at him. "My metalsmithing is not lacking."

"Oh, is that right? Then you are a member of the guild? I didn't see any certificates of their approval displayed." He leers at me, daring me to disagree.

Oooh, no, he did *not* just ask me that.

"You know what, sir? I think maybe you're better off enchanting your own dragon sapphires, if you should even find a vein. Everything I've read said dwarves are inexplicably bad at divining the location of that particular gem." I flutter my eyelashes, slightly surprised at the strength of my rage. "Diamonds, gold, silver, sure, you all can find that easily enough. Commonplace, actually. But the truly rare dragon sapphire?" I make a long hum in the back of my throat. "Dragon sapphires are harder for your kind, aren't they?"

"Well, I don't know where you get off talking to me—"

"Not in the guild," I say airily, waving a hand, my cheeks hot with annoyance. "I don't have anyone to answer to, do I? I'm a free agent. I can talk to you however I want. And since you've come into my shop, critiquing my work, I don't think I'm in the mood to entertain any more of your insults. Best wishes finding the dragon sapphire," I croon at him as he turns the crimson shade of a beet. "I'll be sure to keep you in my thoughts during what I'm sure will be a fruitless search."

He huffs so hard his mustache blows up, the little bit of his brown eyes I can see absolutely slitted with rage.

"Toodaloo," I say, waving my fingers. "You can go out the way you came. Have a lovely day."

He stares at me in indignation for another long moment, and I just keep smiling at him, feeling completely unhinged.

The moment the door closes behind him, I collapse onto the soft chair in the corner, drumming my hands along the arms in high agitation.

Fuck the guild, fuck that dwarf, and fuck everyone who's put these insane rules into place.

A slip of paper falls from my pocket as I stand up abruptly again, and I stoop to pick it up, unrolling it and reading the words I wrote on it last night.

Be so good no one can ignore you.

Enchanting a range of dragon sapphire-encrusted jewelry would, in fact, fit that goal quite nicely.

My eyes land back on the geology book on the counter, and when a trio of dwarves walk through the door, I barely glance at them.

"We're closed," I yell out. "Closed until further notice."

"Your sign says open," a dwarf says in a brogue so thick I hardly understand him. Like the first dwarf, he's also trembling.

I arch an eyebrow. "The sign says closed." A small gust of magical will, and the wooden placard swings itself around.

The dwarves freeze for a moment, then scurry back out the door.

It takes a few strides for me to lock the door, and I know exactly what I need to do.

I need a guide to the deep, dark places around Wild Oak Woods, and I need to find that dragon sapphire before the condescending dwarves get their hands on it.

And then I need to do what I do best: craft the finest enchanted jewelry on the continent.

There's only one problem I can think of: convincing a certain Unseelie fae to accompany me on my quest.

Good thing I'm a witch, and good thing I have just the thing to coerce him into my service.

Slightly unsavory, sure.

Desperate times and all that.

Fenn pads down the stairs, and I whirl around to face him. "Hope you had a good nap, Fenn, because we have supplies to buy and a trap to set."

But first, I need to grab the blueberry scones from Piper before she sells out.

CHAPTER THIRTEEN

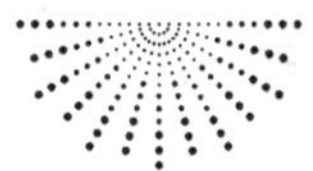

WREN

The Pixie's Perch is busy despite the odd afternoon hour, patrons lounging in the little mismatched tables while Piper packs orders with a smile behind the main counter.

A low baritone voice trickles through the sounds of quiet conversation from the back kitchen, and I blink in surprise as I realize the orc, Ga'Rek, is the one singing. A singing orc. Who is making pastries.

Will wonders never cease?

"Wren!" Piper's voice pulls me back to my purpose in coming here, and I march up to the counter, hoping I haven't waited too long to be able to snag the scones for my new brownie friend.

"You're busy," I tell her, then wince at my needless observation.

"It's been steady today," Piper agrees. "What can I do for you?"

"Do you have any blueberry cheeriness scones left?"

"The ones with the spiced walnuts?" she asks, already heading to the shelves weighed down with sweets. "You're in luck, we've got three."

"I'll take them all." Luck. That's what I need. "Do you have anything with luck spells?"

She glances up at me, her brow wrinkled. "I do, actually. I baked a tray of lucky lemon squares on a whim this morning. We have two left. Do you want both of those?"

I nod. Two is better than one. "Yes. Yep. I want both."

"Five pastries, good for you. I'll wrap up an extra cookie for an even half-dozen. This one has an alluring charm on it. Perfect if you have an admirer in mind."

"Oh, that would be perfect," I gush. Just what I need. To be alluring and have luck? That's exactly what I need—exactly.

Dragon sapphires, come to mama.

Something in my expression must give away my thoughts, because Piper's face screws up, and she raises her eyebrows.

"Should I be worried?" she asks, her tone hushed. "What's gotten into you? I saw you walking back and forth early today, and then there were all those dwarves outside your shop…"

"I have a plan," I say testily, rummaging some coin from my pocket. "Oh, do you have any of Nerissa's favorites? I'll take three of those, too."

I flinch as Piper claps her hand three times, startling me.

"The bakery is closed!" she yells, the whites of her eyes showing. I grab for the package of sweets she's been putting together, but she clucks her tongue at me and pulls them away.

Frowning, I cross my arms over my chest. "It's nothing to worry about," I tell her, and my voice sounds whiney even to my ears.

"It's nothing to worry about, is it?" she says, her voice rising steadily.

The few patrons who've been sitting and having peaceful conversations gather their belongings post-haste and wisely scatter.

"Nothing to worry about," she seethes. "I had to hear second-hand from Ruby about how you've been cavorting with brownies, and then you come in here all," she makes a flustered sound, waving her hand at me. "All worked up and ordering enough charmed sweets to set anyone's witchy senses tingling."

I huff, annoyed that she's pegged me so easily.

"Can I get another almond croissant to go?" a centaur interrupts, looking between us hopefully.

"Go away, Edward!" Piper yells. "Now is not the time for almond croissants!"

She points at the door, and it flies open.

Edward sullenly clops towards it, and Piper slams it after him.

"That was rude," I tell her, trying unwisely to change the subject.

"Rude is you acting like you're being entirely unsuspicious when you know I know you better than that. What in the moon's name is going on?"

I blanch. *Not the moon's name.*

Ga'Rek peeks his head out from the kitchen, lavishing a broad smile on Piper. "You need any help, boss?"

"No, and stop calling me boss." She pushes her hair off her face, still glowering at me furiously. "It's Piper, please. Just Piper."

I squint at the blush rising in her cheeks, but she points a finger at me, and I immediately raise my hands in the universal gesture for giving up.

"Are you sure I can't help—"

"No," we both tell the orc at the same time.

Out of the corner of my eye, I see him shrug, and then back away.

"What are you up to?" Piper hisses, her palms smacking on the counter.

Thunder rolls, shaking the windows of her shop, and our staring contest breaks as we look outside.

"That's an omen," Piper says, now pointing that same dangerous finger at the sky outside.

"It's a storm," I say. "Probably."

"It's an omen, and you're going to tell me why you've got a brownie around and why you're headed to Nerissa's."

I pinch the bridge of my nose, annoyed but not really seeing a way out of it at this point.

That's me, slick as can be.

"Maybe you can help me," I finally say. "Hand me a lemon bar."

She sniffs, untucking the paper flap and pulling one of the yellow sugar-dusted squares out.

"It smells heavenly."

"Don't try to butter me up," she retorts. "The charm only lasts two hours so whatever you're planning better be quick."

"I bought two," I say around the bite. "It's really delicious."

"Of course it is. I made it."

"She's the best," Ga'Rek shouts from the kitchen. "I want to know too, for the record."

"No," we both yell back.

"Come on," I say to her glumly, despite the deliciousness on my tongue. "I'll tell you while we walk."

"We're picking up Willow on the way." Piper lifts the counter and dusts her hands on her apron before untying it.

"Good idea," I say meekly.

"What do you need for whatever spell your casting?"

"Who said anything about a spell?"

"You're a bad liar, so just stop. It's insulting me."

"Fine." I throw my hands up and nearly tell her exactly what I have planned before I remember the nosy green orc in the kitchen.

Piper follows my gaze, and her eyebrows shoot even further up her forehead. "Oh no."

I roll my eyes and make my way from The Pixie's Perch onto the street.

"You can't tell him," I warn her as soon as she appears. "You can't breathe a word of it to him."

"What kind of coven sister would I be if I told?" she asks, highly scandalized.

"We're not a coven," I tell her.

"Oh, please. The only thing we're missing is the stamp of approval from those dusty bigwigs who think they have the right to limit us."

It's my turn to be scandalized, and I stare at her open-mouthed. She's never said a bad word about the High Coven, but here she is, looking ready to shoot sparks from her eyeballs.

Thunder rumbles again, and we both glance up at the billowing grey clouds overhead.

"Come on then," I tell her, and we set off at a brisk pace to Willow's greenhouse and apothecary.

"Well?" Piper asks, injecting a world of meaning into the single syllable.

"I have a plan," I say grandly.

A rain drop spatters against the tip of my nose, cold and wet.

"And it involves Nerissa? And closing your store early? And something my new employee can't hear?"

"I am going to bind Caelan to me using a demon trap." The words come out blithely and unbothered despite the fact *actually* voicing them makes me feel sick.

"Why?" She rounds on me, her eyes huge. "Why would you do that?"

I ignore the censure in her voice and walk faster. I also take a massive bite of lemon square to give myself time to consider how I'm going to answer.

"If you think you can get away with eating instead of answering me, you've misjudged my willingness to knock that lemon bar out of your hand."

I glare at her and swallow.

"Because I need an Unseelie fae's help in finding a rare vein of ore, and he's the Unseelie fae I have on hand."

"You could have picked the other one," she says, narrowing her eyes at me. "The one with the wings."

I shrug a shoulder. "I know Caelan better."

"How?" she scoffs.

"We had dinner together last night."

"Oh, and now you've decided you're just going to bind him to your will? After one dinner? He must have been good with his mouth."

"Piper!" I stare at her, aghast. "That's not at all what this is about."

"So he is good with his mouth." She smirks at me.

"That's not what I—no. I mean, I don't know. I don't know! We walked around and he was clever and he has the ability to find the damned gemstones and that's all I need him for, so I can find them, we can mine some, and I can finally get in the goddess-damned guild and make a real go at living my life the way I want." A sharp pain hitches in my chest, and I suck in a breath, suddenly fighting back tears.

"Right," Piper says, nodding her head like she expected nothing less. "Well, in that case, we definitely need Willow."

"And I'm not sorry for it," I continue. "I'll only bind him for a few weeks, you know, temporary, and then I'll unravel the spell and he can be on his merry way doing whatever Unseelie courtiers do."

"He's a *courtier*?" Piper asks, her nose scrunching up.

A flash of guilt sparks in me as I realize Caelan might not have wanted me to tell anyone that.

Another drop hits my cheek, then another, and before I can answer, we're running in the quickening downpour towards Willow's shop.

Panting, we finally tumble through her door, the musky scent of damp earth and vegetation clinging to the humid air inside.

"Oh, you're here," Willow says cheerfully. "I just sent Kieran on his way to avoid the storm."

A dark-haired woman walks into the front of Willow's apothecary from the back room, mist curling around her.

Piper snorts, and I stifle a laugh.

"There you are," Nerissa intones, ignoring Piper's reaction to her dramatics. "I was starting to wonder if you were going to show up at all."

"Right," I say, plunking the box full of pastries down on Willow's counter, ignoring the clear jar of what appears to be rodent feet next to it in favor of taking another lemon square. "Here's what we're going to do."

I launch into my explanation, getting as far as explaining the temporary nature of the binding with Caelan only to see Willow's scowl growing increasingly dark.

"Couldn't you just ask him for help?" she finally interrupts. "Doesn't this seem like a lot of effort when you could just ask?"

"He's an Unseelie fae," I say, my gaze darting around to my friends' faces. "You can't trust their word."

Piper tilts her head, a thoughtful expression on her face.

Willow throws up her hands. "Right. Goddess forbid we treat them like they are capable of a full range of emotions. We'll just bind them to our will!"

Nerissa smiles. "Exactly, Willow. What must be done must be done."

"Oh, stop it, Nerissa. We're all witches. There's no reason to be pointlessly theatric with us." Piper crosses her arms in irritation.

"I'm just saying, there's something more going on here—" Nerissa starts sharply.

"Right, right, and you're the only one who knows about it, as usual." Piper rolls her eyes.

"We don't have all day," I finally blurt, ready to get this show on the road before my willingness to actually carry out my hasty plan disappears. "Let's get this binding started."

"Right." Nerissa rubs her hands together gleefully. "It's spell-smith time."

"I have the spell already," I tell her, trying not to be annoyed. Trying, and failing. "I don't need a new spell."

"I'm just not sure that this is a good idea," Willow hedges. "They're powerful, and it might be nicer just to ask Caelan if he wants to help you."

I swallow the urge to let out a shriek that would make a banshee proud. "Your critique has been noted," I tell her.

"Willow has a point." Piper says, not meeting my gaze.

A disappointed whuff of air sails out of me. "Fine. I can do it by myself."

"Absolutely not," Nerissa says, her voice thick with power. "We do this together. We do this together and we accept the consequences of the magic."

Piper covers her face with her hands, clearly unimpressed by Nerissa.

"Isn't this kind of like a coven thing?" Willow asks, cringing.

"Well, put 'establish a coven' on the to-do list, Willow!" I bellow, out of patience.

That's what I get for waking up early from a brownie invasion and trying to be extroverted all day. An absolutely spent capacity for peopling.

"Oh, I can do that," Willow says brightly. "I'm so glad we're going to start a coven."

I rub my temple, a headache starting to form.

"Hands," I say crisply, and we all link hands and I begin weaving the beginnings of the binding spell that will call Caelan to us… and hopefully keep him under control.

And then I'll get my damned dragon sapphires and finally, finally prove I'm good enough to be in the goddess-damned guild.

CHAPTER FOURTEEN

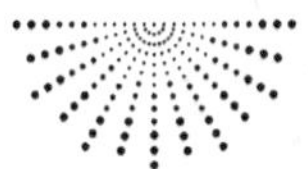

CAELAN

I'm midway through a very satisfactory evening nap when a strange tingling sensation in my midsection rouses me from dozing.

I bolt upright, sucking in a breath of surprise as the tingling grows stronger, more insistent, like something's hooked deep inside my ribs.

"Must be the after effect of dealing with dwarves," I mutter. "Bad for digestion."

I start to lie back down, frowning to myself, when the sensation turns deeply unpleasant, pressure rising all around me. My eardrums begin to thrum, drum-like and distant, but growing faster, louder.

I close my eyes, trying to blot it all out, and when I open them again, I'm no longer in my paltry rented room at the most threadbare inn known to the world.

Dizzy, I do my best to stand up, slightly concerned and very annoyed at my new circumstance. Mist and fog curl around my legs, the scents of wherever I am overpowering and strong: the wet growth of a forest floor, many, many magical ingredients, burning incense, and, strangely, lemon bars.

The stamp of the magic that's brought me here is familiar, and at first, my stomach swoops—but it's not the Dark Queen's.

A lazy smile tugs up my lips as the steamy vapor around me begins to dissipate, because I recognize that magic.

"Well, little Wren, my golden witch. What a surprise to be summoned like this," I purr into the darkness. Light blooms around me in a half-sphere, and at that, my eyes do widen in surprise. Yellow ribbons of power crisscross all around me, interspersed with vermillion streaks, verdant emerald threads, and an improbable candy-coating pink spliced throughout.

"A binding spell," I hiss, my eyes flashing. "Little witch, if you wanted my body, all you had to do was ask."

"I told *you* you should have just asked," a voice whispers, but it's not my Wren. Another witch, then. Has my mortal outcast found a coven, then?

Not that I care.

"I wanted to be certain," a stubborn voice says, and I grin sharply because I recognize that voice.

"Say my name," I command silkily, aroused in spite of my predicament, or maybe because of it, because this little golden-haired witch has outmaneuvered me. *Me.*

The bargainer, the rogue, the knave of the Dark Queen's court.

And I love it.

"You're not the one who determines how this conversation goes, Caelan." Wren sounds miffed, and when her lovely little face comes into view, she looks it, too. Pink-cheeked and flush with power, her eyes very nearly glowing in the dim light.

My breath catches, the tingling under my ribs coming back full force.

A good, solid binding spell, then. *Good for her.*

Pride fills me on her behalf, even as annoyance at being summoned and bound flares anew.

"And yet you said my name so prettily anyway," I tell her, grinning widely. "To what do I owe the pleasure of another night of your company?"

"Another night?" one of the witches in her circle gasps.

"That's right, she didn't tell you? Naughty Wren, the little bird who caught a fairy in a cage of colors." I gesture to the strange shape all around me.

It's a nice bit of a magic, but I'm fairly sure I could break it.

Might hurt though. Probably not worth it.

Besides, I'm curious to a fault.

"Stop making it sound so…" she sputters, trying to put a name to whatever it is she thinks I'm doing.

"Delicious?" I supply, winking outrageously.

She glares at me, and I file the expression away for later. Wren is proving to be even more fun than I imagined in my wildest daydreams.

Well, that's not true, not entirely. I have a very vivid imagination.

"Risqué?" I press. "Intimidating? Delightful? Promising?"

"Illicit!" she snaps. She folds her arms across her chest, pressing her breasts up, and my gaze dips to the soft, round shape of them. A pale expanse of lightly freckled skin, the hollow dip of collarbones at her throat, and that smooth column of her neck.

Perfect for sinking teeth into.

"Illicit sounds like a fun place to start," I drawl, then raise an eyebrow. "Is this your idea of a good time, then? I'm not usually into games of being dominated, but I suppose I can make an exception if that's where your predilections lie."

One of the witches holding the binding spell laughs quietly. Red, I think, from the way the color jangles against the others.

"I see why you like him," the red witch says in a quiet, amused murmur.

"That is not, I do not like him, that's not why we—"

"Enough of the foreplay, Wren. Do you want to join me in here or am I meant to show you my fae parts as an exhibition?" I know full well that's not why she's put me in her silly bubble, but I can't say I mind the way she screeches in outrage as I start to tug on the hem of my shirt.

"You don't want me to strip down first? Alright, dealer's choice, let me just—"

Before I can whip my cock out, she stops me, her power ramming into me in a heady wave.

"I am bound to do your bidding," I tell her drily.

She juts her chin out, the stubborn little thing, and pouts.

Pouts! As if I asked her to put me here.

I hold back a laugh, highly amused, but unwilling to irritate her further.

For the moment, at least.

"I insist you take me to find a vein of dragon sapphire and do your best to help me bring it safely back to my store, without subterfuge or ill will towards me."

Out of all the things I thought my sweet golden witch would say, that was not among them.

She forced my hand.

Before I could trap her into going with me to beat the damnable dwarves to the dragon sapphire, she trapped *me* into going with *her*.

Stunned, I can only stare at her.

Blonde hair glows in the light of the magic sphere, shining and glossy and begging to be pulled while her mouth opens against mine. Green shoes in mint condition peek out from under a pair of linen trousers that reveal more than they conceal, a fact I like very much.

"You changed your hair," I croak.

Her hand goes to the cascade of it before she remembers she's supposed to be the one in charge and it falls away.

Too bad.

I'd like to see her touch herself.

Everywhere.

"Well? Do you agree to accompany me?"

"Of course," I tell her, and it's completely sincere, for once in my very long life. "All you had to do was ask." I motion to the bubble around me. "This is a nice bit of insurance though, I suppose."

"And you're not going to try to double-cross me or hurt me?"

"Why would I?" I counter.

Keeping her on her delicate little toes while we spend lots of time together on the road is going to be fun. So much fun with this lovely, surprising creature.

"I can hardly stand the excitement of planning for our journey," I tell her as she continues to glare at me, as if this entire endeavor was all my doing.

A laugh threatens, but I push it down.

"We'll leave tomorrow morning," she says tartly. "I expect you packed and ready at dawn."

"Perfect," I purr. "I can't wait to spend day after day in your company, golden Wren."

"It's not, that's not—"

"Of course, I'm truly looking forward to seeing what you have in mind for your newly bound fae," I motion to myself, "at night. Mmm. And just as it's getting cold out. You sly minx. Don't think I don't see straight through you."

"I will see you at dawn." Her voice cracks like a whip, and I can tell I've pushed her just a bit too far.

"Begone, Caelan of the Underhill," she finishes.

And just like that, I'm back in my bed, wide awake, and afire with delight.

What an *excellent* turn of events.

CHAPTER FIFTEEN

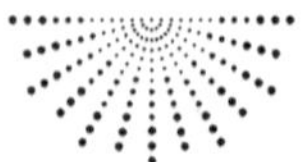

My hands shake as I set the blueberry and spiced walnut scone (with required cheeriness spell) out on the nicest piece of china I have. Gilt-edged, a pink wreath of flowers and vines around the outside and so thin I'm afraid my trembling hands will be the end of it.

A teacup full of milk and a sugar cube follows, because if I'm going to entice the brownie to stay, then I'm going to do my damndest to make sure they want to be here.

Once I'm done setting out the sugary feast, I retreat to my room and collapse face first onto my bed.

"What a day," I moan, the words muffled by soft bedding.

I set out to find more people in town to network with, and I checked that off the list early, basically overwhelming my social barometer right off the bat. Then I worked on new enchantments and the physical work of goldsmithing.

Then I got into an argument with a dwarf.

Then I bound an Unseelie fae to do my bidding until we bring home the dragon sapphire or die trying.

I flop onto my back, my feet hanging off the edge of the bed. A few nudges of my toes and the brownie-crafted green leather shoes topple to the floor.

I bound an Unseelie fae to me.

Now he has to do my bidding, until I see fit to unbind him.

I would feel terribly guilty about it, if he hadn't been such a complete asshole as soon as he appeared in that bubble.

What happened to the clever, funny, and kind man I walked around town with last night?

I *should* feel guilty.

It's worrisome that I only feel irritated and out of sorts about the whole thing.

The bed squeaks as Fenn hops onto the mattress, padding silently across the yellow quilt until he reaches my chest. A rough paw pats my cheek, and I crane my neck to look at him.

"I think I might have made a mistake," I tell him somberly.

His amber eyes regard me seriously, and then he curls up at my shoulder in his cinnamon bun fashion, a cozy fur against my skin and his comforting heartbeat in my ear.

My jaw pops as I heave a massive yawn, and I stare up at a growing water stain on the ceiling from what must be a leak in the roof.

Another expense I can't afford. Without business, I won't be able to even keep this place, no matter how I came into it.

I need the damned dragon sapphires, and I need the guild to back me, and I don't give a damn if I hurt Caelan's feelings by binding him to my task.

Well, maybe I do give a damn… but at least this way I can guarantee myself a future here in Wild Oak Woods.

I don't want to leave.

I suck in a breath through my nose as the realization hits me full force.

I want this place to be home. I want to make it one.

I have a plan, and I'm damn sure I'm going to make it happen, because no one else can do it for me.

CHAPTER SIXTEEN

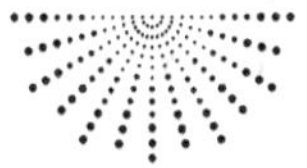

CAELAN

$\mathcal{D}$aybreak is not my finest hour. Never has been, never will be. I'm fairly certain the Dark Queen outlawed daybreak centuries ago in the Underhill for the same reason.

Still, I'm outside the conniving little witch's shop as the sun begins to peek across the horizon, a pack on my shoulders and a sneer on my face.

It wouldn't do to let Wren know just how much I'm enjoying the fact that she not only managed to bind me to her, but also was bright and devious enough to see an opportunity to best the dwarves and help herself.

It wouldn't be nearly as fun if she knew I wanted to trap her into this exact situation, anyway.

I whistle tunelessly, my hands jammed in the pockets of the sturdy workpants Druze lent me when I made my way back to Long Leaf Brews with an explanation of why I wouldn't be there the next few days, or weeks, even.

Silent and stoic as ever, the huge dryad managed to fill up a pack of supplies for me as well as provide clothing more amenable to the journey Wren and I are about to go on.

As for Lila, she gave me a quick hug and told me to come back in one piece.

I find I like both of them much more than I should.

Dreadful idea.

I raise my hand to knock at the door to Witchwork's Jewelry, slightly concerned that I haven't seen my minx of a witch yet, when I smell it on the air.

A fucking fae.

A fucking Seelie Court fae, too.

Rage stiffens my back, and my eyes narrow as I peek into the shop windows, intent on finding the source of the offending stench. It's empty, though, as far as I can see, but that awful rosehip and lilac perfume doesn't lie.

There's a Seelie fae in there somewhere.

"Right on time," a voice chirps from behind me.

I bang my head into the window, startled by the words.

Wren stands there, in fitted breeches that curve around her thighs and show off a plump ass ripe for squeezing.

"Did I scare you?" she asks, her hand fluttering to her chest as though I've managed to startle her, too.

"I am *never* scared," I tell her stiffly, then dip at the waist in a perfunctory bow. "What's the plan, oh mistress mine?"

"I didn't mean to offend you," she says mildly, eyebrows arched. The dawn breaks across her golden hair, combed and shining, piled into a fountain that spills down her back. "What were you looking for in there, anyway?"

"I smelled something disgustingly floral."

"Hm." She lifts one shoulder, then waves a book at me.

I tilt my head, regarding the wicked minx before me. Not nearly wicked enough. Not yet, anyway.

I'd start by pulling that deep green blouse from her body, and kiss my way down her chest, paying special attention to her breasts. What color will her nipples be? Pink like the inside of a conch shell? Sandy brown? Or maybe some strange color like the dryads and nymphs I've wet my cock in.

I'll have her begging for the same by the end of this, and the thought brings a real smile to my face.

"What?" she asks warily.

"Just thinking about how I'm going to undress you and make you my plaything."

"Stop that at once," she says with a sniff, opening the book in her hand and displaying a map.

I lean closer, peering at the watercolor rendering of Wild Oak Woods. "Is this supposed to help us?"

"It's a map." She stares up at me with her big ocean-blue eyes, all innocence and beguiling magic.

It's not a map, it's a trap, but I'm no longer sure who's behind it.

"If you have a map, then why do you need me?"

"I can't go alone," she says, rolling her eyes.

Oh no, she's not getting out of this that easily.

"Right. So you have no one else you could have asked, you just had to bind me to you?"

A consternated noise of frustration burbles out of her throat and I sidle closer to her, loving how easy it is to get her worked up.

"I have to say, little Wren, I'm flattered by all this attention and thought you've given to me," I purr. "You've leveled the playing field between us now. I was on my very best behavior with you the other night, and all that hard work went down the drain when I didn't have to be. What a relief."

Her nose wrinkles adorably.

I lean closer, blotting out the smell of the Seelie fae with Wren's magic scent, dark places and metal and the faint earthy musk of her skin, filling my lungs with her as if I can draw her very essence inside me.

"Are you trying to say you're going to be awful to me just because I've bound you to me?" Her lower lip juts out, and I poke at it until she bats my hand away.

"No, I'm saying I'm done holding back." Irritation flashes through me at her audacity, tempered by the fact that same audaciousness is completely alluring.

"Holding back?"

"I am not some Seelie fae of sunshine and light and butterflies and summertime," I grit out, grasping her chin in between my fingers.

She gasps at the contact, staring daggers at me from those seaside eyes.

"I am of the Underhill. I am made of magic and mischief, and you should have remembered that before you bound yourself to a monster." My fangs extend, the sharp points of them on full display.

Wren sniffs, jerking her chin away. Her fists ram onto her hips as she stares up at me, all defiance and fire. "I've never met a monster who would eat sweets and try to make me laugh."

Warmth spreads across my chest, and my fangs retract.

She pats my chest. "See? Not such a scary Unseelie after all."

Wren turns on her heel and sets off down the cobblestone path, heading straight for the Ever Forest that borders the town of Wild Oak Woods.

Leaving me bobbing after her like some kind of child's toy.

Not such a scary Unseelie after all.

CHAPTER SEVENTEEN

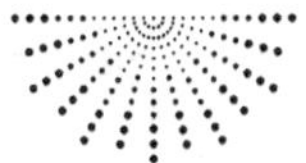

WREN

By the time we reach the first rest stop marked on the map in my new book, I'm in a foul mood.

My feet hurt, the boots the brownie left for me this morning not nearly broken in enough for the type of hiking we're doing.

Sweat drips along my temple, my hair sticking to my cheek.

A fly drones around my ear, and I swat at it with extreme prejudice.

"Not exactly the morning jaunt you expected?" a cool voice asks, and I turn on my heel and glare at him.

Mr. Monstrous Unseelie fae himself looks as fresh as he did when I met him outside my shop this morning, not a hair out of place and as stunningly handsome as ever.

My stomach growls, and I frown at him as I pull out a cookie from my sack.

"Why are you looking at me like this is my fault?" he asks.

I bite into the cookie with more force than necessary, pointedly ignoring his very valid question. "Aren't you supposed to be guiding me? Wasn't that the whole terms of the binding?"

"You haven't asked me nicely," he says with a slick smile.

"Will you guide me?" I grumble, taking another bite. Really, it's a very good cookie—salty toffee bits with huge chocolate chunks, and just crisp enough to be satisfying to bite into. Yum.

"Mmm, that's still not very nice." He's grinning, like this is the most fun he's had in ages, and some of my grumpiness dissipates because how sad is that?

An early morning hike with a very non-morning witch when you've been forced into service.

"Will you please guide me?" I put a little sugar on it.

"Where would you have me guide you?" He bats his eyelashes innocently, and I decide maybe his idea of fun is perverted.

He tilts his head, waiting, and I almost choke on a laugh. I'm pretty sure I've seen a cat with that same expression a time or two.

"Would you please guide me to the dragon sapphire, oh beautiful and terrifying Unseelie?"

He positively preens, smoothing his elegant, long hands down his muscled chest. "Well, I suppose I could. If you share your cookie with me."

I sigh. This is not how the binding is supposed to work.

Ugh.

I break the cookie in what would have been half, were it still whole, and he snatches it out of my hand, gobbling it down instantly.

Okaaaay, then.

With wide eyes and the kind of calm demeanor I reserve for sticky, screaming toddlers and angry cats, I step back and finish chewing.

My skin flushes and I fan my face, suddenly hot all over.

I clear my throat, my entire body tightening up, my stomach swooping strangely. Maybe the cookie isn't sitting right.

I glance back at Caelan, my nose scrunched up, and it hits me like a sledgehammer.

He is so, so, so handsome.

That dark, glossy hair that's begging to be touched, the sharp angles of his jaw and cheekbones… and those eyes.

I sigh, studying him. The powerful, lean muscles under his shirt look positively rubbable, and before I'm even aware of what I'm doing, I've closed the gap between us.

My fingers tug up the hem of his shirt, exposing a breadth of purple skin. A moan slips out of my mouth as I run my hands over his abs, and when I glance up at him, his ice-blue eyes are dilated, his fangs extending.

"You are the most devious, darling creature I have ever set eyes upon," he says in a rasp, and then his hands are at my hips, pulling me closer to him until our bodies connect.

"Kiss me," I tell him. I don't think I've ever wanted someone like I want Caelan.

He does as I ask, and there's nothing sweet or gentle about it. His mouth presses against mine, his fangs sharp against my lower lip. I fit myself against him as best I can, hungry for more, needing all of him all over me.

My hands are pulling at his shirt, and I moan in approval as he breaks the kiss to take it off all the way.

"You're perfect," I tell him.

A snarl leaves his mouth as his arms circle my waist again. My hands travel down the expanse of his back, needing to map every surface of his beautiful body. There are rough ridges all along his skin, but I don't have time to worry about that.

I need more of him, of all of him, and I don't know what's taken me so long to realize just how much I need Caelan.

CHAPTER EIGHTEEN

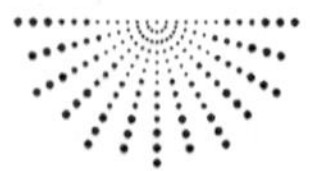

CAELAN

I do not know what's possessed Wren to throw herself into my arms, to let me devour her with my mouth, to hopefully, finally, taste the sweetness between her legs, but I'm fucking grateful for it all the same.

As if I would ever say no to her.

She's especially beautiful like this, eyes glossy with lust, cheeks flushed the prettiest rose, and I don't think I've ever found anything or anyone as alluring as I do this mortal witch.

I take her plump ass in both hands, groaning as I squeeze the soft flesh of it and pull her up. Her legs wrap around my waist, and the feel of her hot cunt against my stomach makes me lose what little control I have left.

"Need you," I tell her, massaging the delicious flesh of that ass. "I want throw you to the ground and plunge my cock so deep inside you, you alluring little minx." I kiss my way up her neck, scraping my fangs across the throbbing vein there, then begin whispering fervently against her ear. "I'm so glad you've finally come to me. I would have waited a century, but this is much better. I will ruin you for other males. Once you have a taste of my cock, you'll be the one bound to me, Wren."

She moans, arching her back, and I run my hands up through her blouse, one arm wrapped around her waist as I kiss her.

I could die for the taste of her, and while I was already certainly bewitched, the tattoos scrolling across my skin telling the tale of our entwined fates, after touching her like this, obsession will be the only way to describe what I feel for her.

Obsessed with the way her fingernails scratch lightly down my back, obsessed with the way her breath hitches when I find the stiff peaks of her nipples.

"Wait," she says, her body stiffening against me, and not in a way that signals pleasure.

I pause, breathing heavily, and do my best to pull my mouth away from the addictive taste of her skin.

"Wait," she says again, and her voice is panicked, that half-lidded look of lust replaced by wide eyes.

It takes all of my self-control, which I admit is not one of my strengths, to set her down.

Early autumn leaves crunch under her boots, and she backs away from me so quickly she rams up against the rough bark of a tree.

It stings. More than stings, it hurts to see her look at me like that, like I'm some kind of disgusting creature instead of the perfect specimen I know myself to be.

"Change your mind, love?" I ask, arching an eyebrow and crossing my arms over the ache in my chest.

"You don't want this," she says, shaking her head, her lower lip trembling. "It was the cookie."

"I do—" I pause, trying to parse her odd declaration. "The what now? Is that what you call this? Is that a witch saying? A cookie?" My gaze drops to the juncture of the thighs which were so deliciously wrapped around me only moments ago.

"Cookie?" I repeat, utterly confused.

"No, don't call it that." She throws her hand down as if trying to shield herself from my view.

"You're wearing pants, love. I can't see it, no matter how much I would like to," I purr, stepping closer to her.

Her eyes go wide, and she holds up a hand. "You don't want me."

"What?"

"The cookie. The cookie we shared, it was charmed from The Pixie's Perch, from Piper. I forgot. It had an alluring charm on it." She pales, clearly so distraught about feeding us both some kind of seduction spell that she doesn't even realize that kind of charm wouldn't work on an Unseelie fae.

My attraction to Wren isn't the result of some silly kitchen witch's spell.

Not even close.

My stomach drops though, because not only does she think it is, that damned cookie is the cause of *her* sudden change in behavior.

My face falls.

Stricken, I step away from her.

"I'm so sorry, I'm so sorry, Caelan, I would never have kissed you otherwise, that was just… a spell. I'm so sorry." She scrapes a hand over her face, looking lost as a little lamb led to slaughter.

And I, the monstrous fae, hold the axe. It would be so easy to paste a smile on, to tell her the feeling has passed.

I glance down at my shirt on the ground, and the thick black tattoo vining across my bare arm catches my attention.

The tattoo that appeared as soon as Wren Tierson walked into my life.

Fate works in funny ways, and I'm sure she's laughing at choosing a mortal witch as my mate.

"The cookie didn't make me kiss you," my mouth says, and I

must look as terrifying as I am terrified, because Wren makes a small squeak of horror.

I could back down, tell her it was all a cruel joke, but I don't want to hurt her.

I want to kiss the pretty lips that form a tight line on her face until she opens for me like a rose in bloom.

"Yes, it did—"

I hold up a hand, and her throat bobs as she swallows. "No, it did not. I wanted to kiss you as soon as I saw you walk through the door of the kitchen witch's café."

"She's not a kitchen—" Her head snaps up. "Wait."

"You know, I think I'm tired of that word," I say on a sigh.

I feel lighter for having told her the truth, at least, part of it.

"But I bound you to me," she insists, looking miserable. "Maybe you're just feeling the spell effects and saying that because I did it wrong—"

"Wren of the gold and jewels," I say softly, shaking my head. "I am bound to you willingly, you little fool. I could have broken your spell the minute you called me, but it suits me rather well to be tied with the object of all my desires. I find that I am unwilling to be away from your side, and you are just as much now bound to me." I spread my hands wide, at a loss for how to further explain my feelings on the matter.

"I, uh," she stammers, pushing a stray lock of golden-blonde hair from her forehead. "I don't know, maybe we can read up on how to break the binding before we fulfill our purpose together."

"No," I say vehemently, and she startles, blinking up at me with those sea-blue eyes. "I'm not interested in breaking the binding. We will find your dragon sapphires, and you will allow me to…" I search for the word, trying to figure out a way to say what I mean.

"Court me?" she asks, a slight hopeful tilt to her lips that makes me want to fucking ravish her.

"Court you until you decide to let me ruin you for all other males and keep you to myself forever," I snarl. "Call it courting if you will."

She simply stares at me, her mouth slightly open in shock, her chest rising and falling rapidly. "Oh."

"Oh," I echo, feeling like more of a complete idiot than I ever have in my long life. I brush my fingers through my hair, then a chill breeze reminds me I'm half-naked in the Ever Forest, and I slip my shirt back on.

"Well," I say expansively. "Shall we continue to search for your sapphires?"

Her pink tongue darts out as she licks her lips. "I didn't know you felt that way."

Her long hair falls over her shoulder as she cants her head up at me, scrutinizing and so adorable I have half a mind to tuck her under one arm and carry her around.

"Now you do," I make myself say mildly, because I know enough about the golden witch to know she would not appreciate being carried around.

"Are you sure it isn't from the cookie?"

"Do you wish it were?" The question slips out before I can think better of it.

It hangs between us for a long moment.

A grey squirrel skitters into the clearing then stops, standing on its hind feet and glancing between us before darting back the way it came, deciding this was not an answer it wanted to stick around and hear.

"No," she says, and it's faint.

I'm selfish enough to take that as her full stamp of approval.

"Good. Then prepare yourself to be wooed."

"Wooed?"

"Wooed." I nod emphatically. "And the first order of wooing is finding your sapphires so that you can achieve your goal. Then I will make you a delicious dinner, rub your feet, which I can tell are hurting, and you'll decide to let me kiss you again."

"I will?"

"Yes." I point through the trees, eyes narrowing. "I think the rocks you want are this way."

I don't wait for her to argue or agree, simply set off in the direction of the tug of jewel ore in my gut.

All things underground belong to the Underhill, and my witch was bright enough to recognize I'd be her best bet in locating the vein of gems.

I always did like a clever girl.

CHAPTER NINETEEN

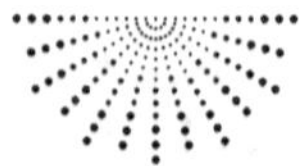

WREN

I am, for once in my life, completely without any idea of what to say or do.

"Maybe we should go back?" I finally venture. I've been trailing behind Caelan with my mind whirling ever since he declared he would be wooing me and ruining me for other men.

Er, males, I suppose, considering he's not a man.

"Because your feet hurt?" he asks, finally pausing, glancing over his shoulder at me.

"Well," I hedge. "Yes. I need the sapphires, but I also need to be able to walk. Maybe together we can pinpoint the location and set out tomorrow with a fresh plan?"

His long legs eat up the ground between us, and before I can adjust to his change in direction, he hauls me into his arms.

Fenn races into view, back from whatever adventure he's been having on his own, and lets out a yowl of outrage.

Caelan laughs softly at the sight, arching one of his flawless eyebrows at my familiar. "He has a lot to say for a small furry thing, doesn't he?"

"It's okay, Fenn," I say, and the fox's hackles settle down nearly immediately. He whines at me, then makes the peculiar chirping noise specific to foxes.

"He's very talkative," Caelan tells me.

"You don't need to carry me," I say, but there's not a lot of heart in the statement. My heels are nearly raw from the backs of the stiff leather boots, and the thought of walking all the way back to town is enough to make me want to lie down on the forest floor until the moss grows over my body.

"I don't need to," he repeats, huffing slightly. "What part of me courting you did you not understand?"

My face screws up as I consider his question. "Most of it?"

"In that case, this will be an incredibly easy process." He huffs in amusement, icy blue eyes narrowing as he glances down at me. "It would help if you put your arms around my neck."

"You don't seem to be struggling."

"Mm. Maybe I just want to be closer to you."

My hands are sitting awkwardly in my lap now, so I do as he suggests and loop them around his neck, my cheeks heating as our skin makes contact. Just moments ago his hands were on my breasts, his mouth against mine, and I would have let him do anything he wanted with me.

"I'll have to have a word with Piper about that cookie. She said it was an alluring spell. That was much more than that."

"Did you consider maybe you're just attracted to me?" A smile slants his lips, softening his entire face. "I think the cookie just gave you an excuse to do what you already wanted to do."

I blink. "Is that right?"

He doesn't answer though, just makes a small, amused sound in the back of his throat.

I study him as he walks. He hardly makes any noise moving

over the ground, the crunching leaves and cracking branches that marked my clumsy footsteps now absent.

FENN PRANCES ALONG BEHIND US, his white-tipped fluff of a tail high in the air, making me smile.

"You love that little creature," Caelan says, and when I glance up, his gaze is on my face, steps as quiet as ever.

"Of course I do," I say, slightly surprised by the comment.

"How does it work?"

"Witches' familiars?"

"Yes. I don't know much about it." He looks annoyed by the fact that he doesn't know, and I realize it must take a lot for a cocky fae to admit they don't know something.

"When witches are ready to take a familiar, to level up their craft, typically, they begin to seek one. It's different for every witch." I smile, remembering the morning I found Fenn curled up at the foot of my bed. "Fenn came to me, and it was like a piece of my soul and magic I didn't know I'd been missing were suddenly there."

The intensity of his attention grows. "I know the feeling exactly."

I don't know how to respond to that, so I forge ahead to satisfy his curiosity. "There is a shop in Wild Oak Woods that caters to witches who need assistance finding the best familiar for them, or need help with their familiar, or want to take a secondary familiar. The witch who runs it, Rosalina, she's an animal mage. She'd probably be the one you want to ask any in-depth questions."

"So you don't summon them from the realm of hell?" he presses.

"Um, no. Well," I squint, mulling it over as I study the patchy blue sky through the leafy canopy. "I suppose you could. That wouldn't be a familiar though, not in a regular sense. That would be more like shadow magic."

"Evil?"

I blow out a breath, suddenly uncomfortable with the discussion. "You know, intent is what matters for us. Evil is in the intent, not the magic itself. Certainly shadow magic can incorporate darker components, but it just... is. The purpose of the casting determines the morality of it. This isn't my specialty either. I just do jewelry enchanting. I'm a smith, not an expert in magical theory."

"So is anything inherently evil, then?" he asks, a strange expression on his face, different than the typical self-assured smile and confidence.

"I don't know," I say simply. "I think intentions can be evil, yes. I think the will of the caster... or the being, I suppose, is the most important."

"So the Unseelie fae may not all be evil, though that is what most of the above ground world believes?"

My heart aches, my sympathetic streak on full display as I stare up at him, aghast.

"Do you think me evil?" he asks, the question light and breezy.

"I think if you were evil, you would have enjoyed my pain instead of scooping me up and insisting on carrying me home." I shrug slightly, my shoulder brushing against his chest. "I think you wouldn't have come to Wild Oak Woods at all, actually."

"Maybe I just selfishly wanted to hold you close," he says.

It shouldn't make my heart flutter, but it does. "I don't think you would even want *that* if you were evil, Caelan."

His eyes widen as I utter his name, such a small movement that if I hadn't been staring at his face, I wouldn't have seen it.

A silly smile spreads across my face in response, and before I can even think better of what I'm doing, my finger is moving.

"Boop."

His dark eyebrows nearly disappear into his raven-wing hair. "Did you…"

"Yes. You needed a boop."

"I needed a boop," he repeats.

"Exactly." I grin up at him, relacing my fingers around his neck. "Can't be evil if a witch is booping your nose."

"Oh, is that the rule?"

"Yes," I nod. "I can't believe you didn't know that rule already." I heave a dramatic sigh. "Simply stunned you hadn't heard that." My feet throb, and I snuggle closer into him, enjoying the smell of his shirt, his skin.

It's been a long time since I've been close to a man—er, male.

I forgot how nice it is.

And maybe something is wrong with me, but being carried around like I'm a teeny, tiny dainty doll of a person is completely delicious.

"You promise it wasn't because of the cookie?" I blurt, shame pinking my cheeks again.

"If I have to lick your cunt until you orgasm ten times and beg me to stop to prove to you that this has nothing to do with a cookie, then that's what I will do," he growls.

All the breath blasts out of me at that declaration, and I stare up at him. "Is that on the menu?"

"Do you want it to be?"

"Maybe?" I squeak. "Definitely," I add, throwing caution to the wind.

He starts running, the trees blurring by us, and I decide he's definitely, absolutely, in no way, shape, or form evil.

A *real* monster wouldn't be sprinting back to my house to eat me out.

CHAPTER TWENTY

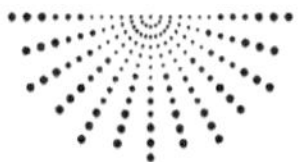

WREN

He's barely broken a sweat by the time he races up to the back door of my shop, Fenn an orange streak behind him, yapping at us both in high distress.

I can't stop giggling, and every time I let out a fresh peal of laughter, Caelan's smile grows and grows.

He finally stops in front of my door, and I try to dislodge myself from his embrace to get my key out.

"Nope," he says. "You're not putting one foot down until we get those boots off and look at the damage you've inflicted on yourself, you stubborn woman."

I let out a little shriek as he easily flips me over one shoulder, a strong arm locking me in place and another digging through the satchel on my back.

When his arm brushes my butt, I let out a little moan.

Caelan stiffens beneath me. "None of that. We will be saving any indulgent activities until after you've been properly cared for."

"What if I want those *first*?" I ask, breathless despite the fact I've done absolutely nothing to warrant it.

"Then you will suffer, I suppose," he says grandly.

The key clicks into place, and then I'm being trundled up the stairs to my apartment, which he also unlocks.

"It smells like you in here."

"I hope that's a good thing," I tell him with a laugh. I'm giddy, lighter than ever, maybe due to the fact I'm not actually standing on my poor feet.

"Your scent was the first delicious thing I noticed about you."

My nose wrinkles. "Is that a fae thing?" I'm not sure I want to know what he thinks I smell like.

I don't need any additional things to obsess over.

"Yes." He sets me down carefully on my favorite chair, a slightly threadbare wingback that was my first purchase when I moved here. It creaks as it takes my weight.

Before I can set my feet down again, Caelan's hands are there. The thick leather laces creak as he unties them carefully.

"What?" I ask, still unable to keep the goofy grin from my face. "Why do you look so upset?"

"It smells like Seelie in here."

"Seelie?" I repeat, confused. "I smell like a Seelie fae?"

"No, not you," he says, his lip curling in disgust at the suggestion. "You smell like dark places deep in the earth, like mystery and magic and gold."

"What does mystery smell like?" I ask, intrigued.

"The question you should be asking is why it smells like Seelie." He sniffs, his eyes flaring.

I hunch forward, staring into his eyes. "Are you... jealous?"

"No," he scoffs, but his blue eyes dart to the side.

"Yes, you are," I say, throwing back my head and laughing. "You are jealous of a brownie."

"A brownie? That explains why it smells terrible."

"Terrible?" I ask, choking on a laugh. "How can it smell terrible?"

"Smells like wet dog. You know, I thought they went extinct," he muses. "Brownies, that is. I remember when they got up to more mischief with the Unseelie than they did humans."

His lips turn down and he refocuses on the task at hand, taking my boots off. Something about the way he said it seems sad, and I tilt my head, wondering at him.

"How old are you?" I cringe slightly as soon as the question is out there, wafting between us.

Caelan finishes tugging the boot off, silent as he slowly and gently rolls the sock off my aching foot.

"Time has no meaning in the Underhill," he finally answers, gazing up at me with those haunting blue eyes. "But I've seen the rise and fall of queens and kings on your land over... what must be centuries."

I clear my throat. "Right." It's staggering to think about, so I try not to, instead watching him slide his hands down my foot. His touch is feather-light, and still, I hiss as his fingers find the jagged edge of a raw blister.

"I have salve for it, you don't have to do that—"

He cuts me off with a stern look, and I nearly laugh at the expression on his face. "I am wooing you."

"This is part of it? Touching my blisters?"

"Believe it or not, Miss Sassy Witch, most fae, Unseelie or otherwise," he grimaces over the word, as if just mentioning the Seelie Court is distasteful, "care for their... would-be partner."

Would-be partner.

I squint at him.

It sounded like he was fishing for that phrase, like that wasn't the one he wanted, not at all.

I heave a sigh, one of relief, as he begins kneading the bottom of my foot with his knuckles, sinking back into the chair.

"What kind of salve is it?" he asks, studying the sore patch of skin on the back of my foot. His forehead creases in concern, and it literally melts any bit of my heart that didn't quite believe he actually likes me.

"It's in the cupboard over there, green jar, lemon balm, comfrey, and pressed walnut oil."

He makes a face. "Comfrey?"

"I made it myself." I shrug one shoulder. "Why? Do you have a secret ancient fae recipe for some mystical unguent that's better?"

"We use comfrey in poisoned arrows," he says archly.

"In high doses, yes, it's toxic, but I'm not purposefully poisoning myself."

"Is there a healer in this backwater town?" he asks.

"The backwater town where you live?" I huff a laugh at his indignant expression. "Yes, there is, but we don't need to bother her for a few blisters, Caelan."

"Are you in pain?"

"Not right now."

"But you were?" he presses, his eyes narrowed as he scrutinizes my face.

"You carried me home," I say, suddenly exasperated with him. "I hardly had the opportunity to be in pain."

"Why are you saying that as if I've deprived you of some noble quest to rub your feet raw?"

"The salve I have will be fine," I mutter mutinously, but he just laughs.

"You deserve the best. Comfrey in some homemade salve is not the best."

"I am a witch! I have healing training!" I cross my arms over my chest petulantly, but he just grins.

"You are a goldsmith and an enchantress of jewelry, and an excellent one at that. You are *not* a healing witch."

"Fine," I say, genuinely interested in an alternative. The salve I made is fine, sure, but I'm not self-absorbed enough to think there isn't a better salve out there. "What do you suggest?"

He picks up my other foot, slowly unlacing the ties and removing the boot and my sock just as carefully as he did the first.

"Well, for starters, I suggest not wearing these boots until they're broken in, and secondly, I suggest you sit back and relax while I make us lunch, a fire, and a healing salve my mother taught me when I was just a young whip of a thing."

"I don't want to put you to any trouble—"

"Oh, really," he purrs, leaning close enough that I feel his breath against my lips. "And that's why you bound us together? So you wouldn't put me to any trouble?"

My jaw drops, and I snort in indignation.

Calean leans further forward, and for a split second, I think he's going to kiss me again.

Then he boops my nose with his finger.

"That's what I thought, Wren Tierson."

With that, he gracefully stands and makes himself fully at home in my kitchen and house. It takes him no time at all to build a fire in my hearth, and even less time than I thought possible to whip up some concoction—that smells much better than my comfrey salve—and gently apply it to my heels.

"There," he finally announces, looking beyond pleased with his handiwork. "Now I can fetch us lunch. I assume your larder is as meager as the rest of your supplies?"

"I have been meaning to stock up on some things," I mutter, slightly abashed.

"No, don't look like that, little witch. I know it's hard for you right now, all of this to manage on those slim shoulders with no one to help. I will be back before you know it."

The door closes softly behind him.

I blink, surprised at the one tear that trickles down my cheek at feeling seen by someone for the first time in a very, very long while.

CHAPTER TWENTY-ONE

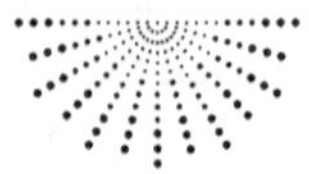

WREN

By the time Caelan returns, I've dozed off in the chair, the crackling fire and soft cushions too cozy and snug to resist.

"Good," he murmurs in my ear, then leans closer to kiss my temple. "I'm glad you've been resting."

I crack one eye open, stretching deliciously long.

His gaze drops to my breasts, and I hold back a laugh, torn between liking how he's staring at me and wondering how in the world he could *ever* think himself evil.

"What's in the bag?" I settle on asking instead. Might be cowardly to ask that instead of something meaningful, but at least it's safe.

The paper rustles as he sets it down on the wooden kitchen counter, and I perk up as he pulls out a few wax-paper-wrapped packages. They fill the small space of my home with a flavorful smell, my mouth watering almost immediately.

My stomach growls in response, and Caelan arches an

eyebrow at me. "You don't take very good care of yourself, do you?"

"I…" I tilt my head and screw up my mouth, because honestly, he's got me there. "I brushed my hair last night."

"I noticed."

"I have a business to run, and I have to do it all myself— The plates are in the left cupboard, no, not that one, yes, right there."

He pulls the plates out, looking so at home in my kitchen that it's hard to believe this is the first time he's been here.

I like the way he looks here.

"I noticed that too," he says, grinning as he piles a plate high with food for me.

Roast chicken with crispy golden skin, dripping with fat and herbs. Fried potatoes with some kind of spicy-looking red sauce. A hunk of fresh sourdough bread with honey butter, still steaming slightly from the oven. Then there are a number of roasted vegetables, a rainbow of carefully sliced moons.

"Where did you get all this?" I ask, absolutely stupefied by the luxury.

"The inn I'm staying at offers lunch and dinner twice a week. This just happens to be the day they offer it."

"You're staying at the Wild Oaks Inn?" I take in the feast he's brought. "And they serve that?"

"If what you're trying to say is, Caelan, I simply cannot believe you're staying somewhere so disgusting, it must be trying for your delicate fae sensibilities, the answer is yes, it is horrible and I am terribly afflicted by it."

I laugh and he grins, continuing his diatribe with gusto.

"And if you're also remarking on how such a run-down place can offer up such a delicious spread, I am just as confused as you are." He crosses over to the chair, scooping me out of it without so much as a warning and gently depositing me at my worn table. "The owner is an old man, mortal human, just regular old fellow, yes? You've met him?"

I nod. Hash Beauchamp is a bit of a legend around here, cranky and stooped with age, but proud and warm once you get to know him.

"Did you know he has a dog?"

"No, I didn't," I tell him.

He slides the plate in front of me, shaking his head as he fixes himself a plate. "He does, he has this dog who might be even older than he is. Grey muzzle, a limp, all that. The dog's name is the real point of interest, though."

"Is it?" I ask, barely able to contain my preemptive laughter.

"The dog's name is Boner." He gives me a meaningful look. "The first night I stayed there, all I heard for the first hour upon cleaning the postage stamp of a room I rented was the old man yelling, 'HERE BONER, WHERE IS MY BONER,' over and over and over again."

I cough, choking on a potato as I laugh. "No."

"Oh, yes, yes indeed. I truly had to sit on the bed once I'd evicted all the spiders from the dark corners and ponder how, exactly, I managed to come to that point in my life."

I manage to swallow the potato, my shoulders shaking as I laugh. "I honestly don't know if I believe you. Hash Beauchamp has a dog named Boner?"

"I asked him about it, you know, once I realized it was in fact, the name of his dog and not some malfunctioning body part." He shivers dramatically, cutting his portion of chicken into neat pieces. "He said the dog just loves to chew on bones. That's why he named him that. I'm not sure he even knows slang."

"There's no way he doesn't." I can't stop laughing, and I'm afraid to eat another bite and choke. I gather all my courage and stuff a massive piece of sourdough dripping with honey butter into my mouth, though, like a real soldier.

"Who could say? Mortals are a strange group." He shakes his head again and takes a bite.

I nod emphatically, because yes, we *certainly* are.

"Does Hash cook the food? This chicken is," I don't have a word to adequately describe it, and I flounder along for a moment before Caelan comes to my rescue.

"It's perfect, isn't it? And no, I had the same question, but he doesn't. There's an elf who works the kitchen. He's not my biggest fan," he adds with a laugh. "But he does good work. I'm glad you're enjoying it."

We both dig into our meals with gusto, falling silent with the sound of clinking forks on china and the crackling hearth as a somewhat musical accompaniment.

"It means a lot to me," I tell him shyly, blotting my mouth with a napkin. "You taking care of me and bringing me this meal."

"It should," he agrees.

I snort, amused all over again at his cockiness. "And why should it?"

"Because I see how little you expect from the world around you. You expect people to tell you no, you expect to fail at this business, in spite of how good you are, because that's what the people around you have taught you to expect. They've failed you."

"Oh." He's rendered me speechless, and he's not done.

"I won't." Caelan delivers this promise with such certainty that it takes me aback.

"We've only just met."

"True."

"How do you know you won't get tired of me? You barely know me."

"My species has been around since the world was learning to crawl, and yet the things your kind and others above ground dream up are both baffling and beautiful all at once. I know I won't get bored of you because you're the only one that matters to me now."

It's an odd speech, both comforting and strange. He says he knows what he wants, and that I believe, because a fae of his age must know himself better than anyone.

But I also know myself, and I'm hardly a prize.

"I get cranky when it's too hot out. I hate sweating."

"Go on," he says, a mildly amused expression on his face as he sits back and studies me.

"I don't like to clean. Or cook. I'm not a good cook, either. I like to knit in my spare time, of which there is none, and read, and snuggle with Fenn by the fire. I like my socializing in small doses and get overwhelmed easily in large crowds. I've been kicked out of a coven and the jeweler's guild refuses to acknowledge the caliber of my work, so I might also be destitute soon without a steady flow of business from them."

He nods, spearing a potato and hefting it into his mouth.

"I get so involved with my work that sometimes I forget to eat or brush my hair, and I like to be right." I peer at him, waiting for him to turn tail and go running. "I let Fenn sleep on the bed with me."

"That's a deal breaker," he says smoothly.

I bristle.

"I'm not shooing Fenn out of my—"

"I'll have to make sure you're fed and your hair is brushed then. Come on, no time like the present to get started."

"But, but—"

"Wren, I'm out of patience for this laundry list of your so-called failings. You smell right to me, you are the most beautiful thing the sun has ever kissed with its morning light, and I want you." He arches an eyebrow, taking our empty plates and washing them in the sink, then disposing of all the trash from our meal while I look on in utter shock.

No one's ever said anything like that to me before.

Sure, I've had guys tell me I'm pretty, and from a scientific perspective I can agree that my face is pleasingly symmetrical and my skin, while prone to breakouts near the full moon, is still smooth and clear at thirty-two.

But to be spoken of like that?

That's new.

Well, a woman could get used to that kind of thing.

I stand up, coming up behind where he's rinsing his hands with the pitcher of cold water, and wrap my arms around his back.

He stiffens at the sudden touch, then slowly turns, looking down at where I've plastered myself to him.

"Thank you," I mumble, the words somewhat lost in the fabric of his shirt.

"It's what you deserve," he says, looking surprised.

"Take me to bed," I tell him.

I don't have to say it twice.

CHAPTER TWENTY-TWO

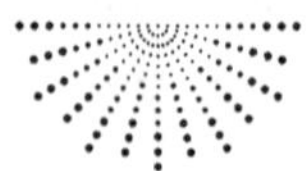

CAELAN

*H*er bedroom smells even more like her, the mouth-watering scent of it driving me wild as I lay her down on her yellow bed.

Yellow bed, blonde hair, my little golden witch.

Blue eyes wide, she's so lovely as she looks up at me, her rose petal lips parted.

"I must be the luckiest male in the history of the world," I tell her, and her skin flushes pink with pleasure at the compliment.

I brush a fingertip across her cheekbone, savoring the warmth of her skin, committing the quality of her small sigh to memory.

Her bed creaks as I put a knee on it, and I raise an eyebrow in alarm.

I'll have to figure out a better bed for us.

She watches me, practically vibrating with nervousness or excitement, I'm not sure, and I lean down, kissing her softly, until she loops an arm around my neck and the fragrance of her arousal perfumes the air.

My cock surges against my pants, near painful with need.

"Are you alright?" I ask, not wanting to push her past her comfort, wanting to take our time together, to move us forward instead of back.

Even if it will fucking *kill* me to wait.

"Mm-hmm," she moans, chasing my lips with hers until I laugh and kiss her again.

She's so soft, everywhere, from the curves of her breasts to the rounded swell of her belly and hips, soft and soothing to all my hard edges.

Wren fits against me perfectly, not nearly as tall as a fae but tall for a mortal, and deliciously, deliciously submissive in bed. A fae female would be challenging me for dominance, trying to wrestle me to the bottom, but Wren is different.

She's happy to let me lead, to let me take my time kissing her, my reverence for her growing with every caress of her skin, her lips. Every tiny sound she makes spurs me on, seeking a new moan or gentle gasp from her.

"You're going to drive me crazy if you don't hurry up," she finally says, her eyes glassy with lust, her palms pressed against the plane of my chest.

I snort. "For someone lying there so sweetly, you sure like to think you're in charge."

"Please," she says, batting her eyelashes prettily at me.

My own eyes close and I groan, unable to keep my hips from snapping against her. Goddess, she'll feel so fucking good wrapped around my cock.

She lets out a low noise of encouragement, her eyes rolling back as she arches into me.

"So you're ready for me to ruin you for other males? To be satisfied by no one but me?"

She half sits up on her elbows, narrowing her eyes at me. "You talk a big game for someone who's still wearing all their clothes."

I growl, pulling my clothes off as fast as I can, and the little minx has the audacity to laugh, covering her lovely smile with a hand as I strip.

"Like what you see?" I ask, gesturing to myself. My cock bobs, as if also asking for approval, and she huffs a laugh as she nods.

"Oh, I very much like what I see," she says, my little witch as bold as brass as she wets her lips.

Before I can ask her to undress, too, she begins to tug at the waist of her pants, slowly pulling them down one leg, then the next, her undergarments disappearing with them.

I can hardly breathe.

My eyes track across the buttery smooth expanse of her calves, the muscled lines of her thighs and the delicious, light brown curling hair over her cunt. Goddess, the mouth-watering honey-sweet scent of her arousal is too much.

Pre-cum beads on my dick and my entire body goes taut as she spreads her thighs, just a little, trying to balance to pull her blouse off.

Her breasts swing free, and my throat goes dry at the sight of her.

"You are more perfect than I have ever imagined," I tell her, wanting to touch her, afraid to break this spell she's wrought over me. Afraid that if I so much as move before she invites me to, I'll wake up back in the Underhill and this will all have been a dream. "I always wondered what you would look like when I finally found you, and even my wildest imagination couldn't have competed with the reality of you."

She blushes so deeply at my praise that her chest goes red, and a low growl ripples out of me, my fangs lengthening.

Slowly, I curl my hand around my cock, unable to keep from touching myself with such a vision before me, and pump my hand down it.

Wren's gaze drops from my face to my cock, so fucking hard for her already, and when she bites her lip, I physically ache to touch her.

"Tell me what you want," I force out, refusing to move before she asks me.

I might ruin her for other males, but she's already ruined me, and I haven't even tasted her yet.

CHAPTER TWENTY-THREE

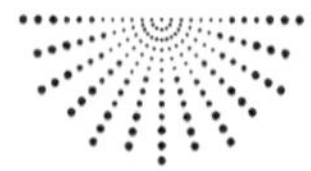

WREN

The sound of my heart is a hammer in my ears, my entire body keyed up and ready for Caelan.

"I want you to do what you promised," I finally answer him, feeling slightly shy, despite the fact that we're both completely naked, no charmed cookie involved.

He lets out another low rumble, what sounds suspiciously like a growl, and my eyebrows arch as I wait. My thighs tremble, and I can't deny I'm nervous because it's been a while and his dick is… huge.

Purple, a darker shade than the rest of him, closer to eggplant than the light lavender of the rest of his skin, a silvery pearl of liquid drips from the tip and I squeeze my thighs together, anticipating the feel of him.

"Be more specific, little golden witch," he demands, arching a dark eyebrow.

I clear my throat, throwing caution to the wind, deciding to make good on his promise in the Ever Forest.

"You said you'd eat me like a feast." My voice breaks on the last word.

A cocky, stunning half-smile tugs up one corner of his mouth, his fangs lengthening. "So I did."

Growing bold under his hot, steady gaze, I swallow and push my right leg further out.

His eyes dilate immediately, the light blue swallowed up by darkness as I spread myself for him, putting myself on display.

An invitation.

"You didn't ask what eating you like a feast meant," he says, the bed groaning as he puts his weight on it, climbing over my body. My hands go to the thick muscle of his chest, loving the feel of his warm body against my palms, the way he shudders at my touch, his muscles bunching as he moves.

His mouth finds mine, and suddenly, his gentle, exploring kisses aren't enough.

I need more.

My heartbeat quickens to the pace of hummingbird wings, and I run my hands down his back until I find the firmly muscled globes of his ass, and squeeze.

I'm rewarded with a feral snarl, and he nips at my lower lip, fangs sharp and exciting.

"Be careful what you wish for, love, because you might just get it."

"Tell me what you meant by feasting on me," I whine. I can't wait any longer. I can feel the orgasm starting to build, wretchedly out of reach still, and I take one hand off his ass and slide it down my pelvis until my fingers find my slick heat.

I moan, my hips lifting of their own accord as I find my clit.

Caelan's gaze is avid, transfixed on my face, and I lock my eyes on his.

"Touch me," I say, my voice high and breathy with need.

He groans, and then he's moving down my body. His mouth latches on one nipple and I cry out, my circles on my clit growing more fervent as he sucks. He skips the other breast, leaving me wanting for more, but desperate to have him where he's headed.

He leaves a trail of hot kisses down my abdomen, pausing for a long moment to stare at my belly button with abject confusion.

It's only then I realize he doesn't have a bellybutton, but as his attention drifts lower, I shove that thought aside for another time.

His hot breath drifts over my pussy, and I keep touching myself as he watches, his fangs looking longer and sharper than ever.

I'm writhing against my bed, desperate to come and so close, when the steel band of his fingers lock around my wrist and he pulls my hand away from me.

His mouth closes around my wet fingers, and I moan as he sucks them, his long tongue grazing the tips.

"My turn," he rasps, and he presses the palms of his hands to the inside of my thighs, spreading me wide. "Good little witch, you taste so fucking good. I want you to come all over my tongue for me, can you do that?"

He lowers his hot mouth to my sex, and I can't manage a coherent answer as his tongue laps at my clit, his fangs pressing the lips of my pussy wide open and holding them there. I'm crying out his name, my hands fisting in his hair as he works me. He plunges a finger in, stretching me, and my legs begin shaking in earnest.

"What a lovely witch you are, so wet and warm for my cock, so ready to let me stretch you. So tight, such a pretty pink cunt," he murmurs, and each word of praise winds me tighter.

A second finger joins the first, and he's pumping in and out slowly, my pussy making an obscenely wet noise.

"You taste like the nectar of the gods. You are a fucking dream, Wren." His hips are grinding against my bed, the entire frame creaking. "Tell me what you want, pretty witch."

"More," I cry out, my hips bucking.

"Ask me nicely," he growls, a feral look in those blue eyes.

"Please, please, Caelan, I need more."

He doesn't make me wait, and as he adds a third finger inside me, he sucks my clit, hard, somehow lapping at it and finding the secret spot deep inside me that makes me scream.

White fire flashes across my field of vision, my body finally reaching the apex, the orgasm so strong that it seems like gold sparks are falling from the ceiling.

"Look at you," Caelan says, still pressing my thighs apart. "Look at how fucking perfectly you came for me," he croons. "Pretty little Wren. Look what you did to me. To the room."

I blink, and sure enough, there are gold sparks in the air, dazzling and ridiculous, proof of my magic's happiness at what we just did.

As for Caelan, he's half-kneeling on the bed, his cock now a deep shade of plum, and thicker than ever.

My jaw drops at the sight of it, and as I watch, it grows.

A bulge forms at the base of his cock, and suddenly, I want to touch it.

I want Caelan to feel as good as I do.

I sit up, slightly dizzy but determined, and take him in hand.

"Fuck, Wren, touch me, yes," he hisses, and I love it. I love how this powerful male is at my personal disposal.

It makes me feel powerful in turn, powerful and slightly wicked as I lean down and draw the tip of his cock into my mouth.

"I'm going to come in that pretty throat of yours if you're not careful."

I back off, licking the proof of his words from his slit, and it's delicious. My eyes widen in surprise because he tastes like an almond cake I once had at a very fancy party back in the city, and I want more.

"Tastes good." Shock is clear in my tone.

"fae cum is nutritious, too." His voice is a croak and he cups my chin, looking deep into my eyes. "You've brought out my knot already, little witch. You've put me under a spell, body and soul."

"Knot?" I ask, breathless, wanting to taste him again, addicted to the taste of him already.

"It will stretch you so good, love. You'll come around my cock over and over again, milking me until you're fat and swollen with my cum. I'll lap it from you with my tongue, and make you eat it so none is wasted."

I moan, and I wonder if he hasn't put me under some kind of spell, because that sounds fucking perfect right now.

"And you'll swell with my babe, and I'll fuck you over, and over, and over again, until all you can think about is how good I taste and how much you want me." It's a near snarl now, and the bulge at the bottom of his cock is pulsing slightly.

"I want it," I tell him, whining slightly, feeling heady and faint with desire.

"You're not ready to take it," he warns me.

I don't like that answer; I don't like it at all. I grab the bulge, the knot, he called it, and squeeze.

He looses a ragged groan, and I grin in triumph before lowering my mouth to his cock and taking him as deep as I can. He hits the back of my throat, the unbelievable sweet taste of him stronger now, and I suck on him hard, one hand on his knot, the other working the long, thick shaft of his rock-hard cock.

"You want my knot, little witch, my Wren?" he asks, his voice deeper than before. The bulge in my hand is growing even bigger, hotter, as I work him, taking him as far into my mouth as I can manage.

"Tell me," he demands. "Tell me yes, and I'll make you mine right now. I'll fill you with my cum and you'll be mine until the end of our days. Is that what you want?"

Maybe I've lost what sense I had left because right now, with him holding my hair in his hand, his cock in my mouth, it's all I want.

It feels right.

It feels like the only possible thing to do.

I let him go with a pop, and instead of answering right away, I back up.

He watches me with a lascivious expression, his cheeks a deeper purple now, his fangs even longer than I think they were before.

Slowly, I keep backing up.

Then I turn away from him, go to my elbows and my knees, and shove my ass high in the air.

"I want it," I tell him. "Give it to me."

"Such a demanding, perfect little love, Wren, what a good mate you are."

Mate.

The word floats between us, and I try to grab at it, to hold it close and decipher it.

But he slams into me, and I scream.

He feels endless, stretching me in a way I'm not sure my body can physically handle. The bulge of his cock, his knot, presses into me, and I startle as I realize it's not even in yet.

"Oh, goddess," I moan, and he pushes my chest gently down until my back is as arched as physically possible, my body completely his to use.

And I love it.

"So fucking perfect, and all mine," he snarls, the words less human-sounding by the second. "All mine, little witch. This perfect cunt belongs to me. You belong to me."

I keen, the noise coming out of me like no sound I've ever made before, squirming and pressing back into him.

His hands reach under my body, and then his finger is circling my clit again, soft, gentle brushes at odds with the ferociousness of his voice, at odds with the force of his knot at my entrance.

"Relax, love, relax," he croons. "Relax and come for me. Come for your fae lover."

The circles on my clit intensify and I jerk, pressing back, feeling like it's too much, and then he snaps his hips again and all the breath leaves my lungs at once.

"There it is, there it is, my golden Wren."

I'm falling apart, falling off a ledge so high I could never see it before, and as he pulls me up, flush to his body, something sharp and unexpected pierces the tender flesh of my neck.

He's biting me.

The orgasm lasts so long that I'm no longer sure where I end and he begins.

CHAPTER TWENTY-FOUR

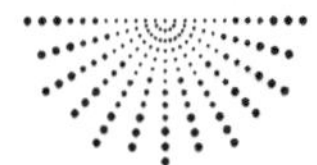

I wake up in Caelan's arms, his knot still holding tight, though somewhat looser than before. I blink, trying to get my bearings, my body as limp and loose and relaxed as it's ever been.

"There she is," he murmurs, pressing a kiss to my forehead, my ear. "I'm going to pull it out now, Wren."

I mumble something completely incoherent and he laughs against the side of my neck, nuzzling a sore spot.

A sore spot from him biting me.

I go hot all over at the memory, and he hisses out a breath as I clench around him.

"Wren, I'm not going to be able to keep it down if you do that," he warns.

Suddenly, I don't want him to. I don't want him to be anywhere but right where he is.

I clench around him again, and his breath cascades across my skin.

"You naughty little witch," he says, fangs scraping my neck again. "You aren't done? I was afraid I'd hurt you. You fell asleep while I came inside you."

"I missed the main event?" I ask plaintively, feeling slightly sad.

He lets out a shocked laugh, his arms tightening around me. "You are a minx. How fucking perfect."

I undulate in his arms, pressing my ass further against him, and he makes a pained noise.

"You aren't going to go anywhere soon if you keep doing that," he warns.

I grind against him, feeling him get harder inside me, harder and thicker, and I grin.

"I don't see the problem with going again."

"You want me to cum in you again," he says quietly, his voice full of wonder.

I pause, thinking about it.

"Maybe I shouldn't?" I finally venture. "I mean, I don't know if we're compatible, but getting pregnant with someone I hardly know—"

I squeak as he grabs my leg, maneuvering in a way I might think was impossible if he wasn't doing it to me, until he's lying on his back and I'm straddling his broad hips, his cock still locked deep inside me, all of its delicious hardness rubbing up right where I need it.

I moan, rocking gently, until I've found the exact spot where I want him.

"Take what you need," he murmurs, and his fingers trace across my cheek. When they meet my lips, I bite them until he laughs.

"What I need," I say, my breath hitching as he moves his hips, his fingers now on my nipples, pinching them. Sensation floods me and I lean forward, starting to move in earnest.

"Tell me," he says.

"I need to know why you said mate," I finally manage, and he sucks in a breath as I bite his nipple, not hard, but enough that he knows I mean business.

"That's what you are, Wren. Mine. I warned you. I told you I'd ruin you, and this is what that means. Mine, you're mine." His hands go to my hips and he pulls me forward, causing me to gasp.

"You can't just say that," I say, but he moves me again and I grip his shoulder, clawlike, as pleasure begins to crest in me again. My fingernails dig into his skin, and he hisses before capturing my mouth with his.

There's a fierce quality to it, teeth and fangs clashing, his hands still moving me over his thick length. I groan as the knot at the base of his cock slides in deeper, my entire body clenching as I climb towards another orgasm, riding him relentlessly now.

I pull back from the kiss and he snarls, his fangs on full display. Bracing my hands against his upper thighs, I move faster, my head falling back.

"I'm not just saying it, you perfect creature. As soon as I saw you, I recognized you for what you are." His mouth settles on my breast.

I'm senseless, moving against him shamelessly, wanting more, greedy with it. With him.

He grazes my nipple with his teeth and I can't breathe, I can't think, and I don't want to. All I want is this, this moment of perfect sensation, of him telling me I'm beautiful and his and the climax that's still just out of reach.

He bites my other nipple, hard, and I scrape my fingers across his back.

My eyes fly open as he changes our positions, drawing me up to him before pushing me back to the bed, asserting dominance.

"So good," I wheeze, the way he slams into me drawing me ever closer, so close.

"So fucking good," he agrees, his eyes never leaving mine. "My perfect mortal witch, made for me in every way."

I want to tell him it doesn't work like that, that witches don't mate, but his clever fingers find the bud of my pleasure again, and all I can do is breathe and climb, climb towards the peak.

"You came to me before I ever thought you would," he growls, his eyes practically glowing in the gloaming dark, the sun setting after our afternoon nap. "You came to me, and then you begged me for my knot, and now you're mine, Wren. Only a mate could do this to a fae."

He might be lying. The thought floats between my ears, but I nudge it away because how could he be?

How could he be, when we fit together like this? When he makes me feel things I've never felt before, and after no time at all? When he drove me to take him into my bed and come inside me?

There's a ring of truth to it, to his declaration that I'm his, and as I come around him again, squeezing his length, fully awake to feel his hot release spurt inside me, I think maybe it's the only truth I've ever heard: that we belong together.

He holds me tight against him, our breathing ragged, our bodies slippery with sweat.

"Tell me you aren't afraid. Tell me you won't run from me, because it doesn't matter where in this realm you go, I would find you and catch you and keep you with me forever."

His gaze is devouring, a slight tremor to his voice that makes my heart ache.

"I'm not afraid." I nuzzle into his neck, breathing him in. "I'm not going to run."

I have a life here in Wild Oak Woods, and I'm not about to give it up because the most handsome male I've ever set eyes on has decided I'm his.

What woman in their right mind would?

"I will prove to you that I will be good to you. A good mate. Please don't be afraid of what I've said, or of me."

He begins moving again, and a moan rips out of me as my exhausted body somehow immediately responds to his.

"I won't run. I don't understand the mate thing, but we have time, right?" I manage to say, his hips moving in slow circles, tweaking my overly sensitive *everything*.

He doesn't answer, kissing me instead.

But if it means more of this… well, I'm willing to figure it out.

CHAPTER TWENTY-FIVE

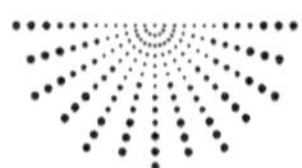

CAELAN

There are two things I notice as soon as I awake.

One, my witch is curled up, content and warm, in my arms, and for that I am thankful.

Secondly, there is a Seelie fae so close that the stench of wet dog overwhelms the scent of my mate, and for that, I could happily kill it.

Unfortunately for my murderous urges towards my distant—extremely distant—cousin of a brownie, my mate seems to like the brownie.

So I hold Wren close, my nose buried in her hair, and I wait for the other fae to leave.

Once it's cleaned the house or mended shoes or whatever other trivial nonsense it's decided to meddle in, I suppose.

Thunder rumbles in the distance, explaining the lack of sunshine streaming through Wren's curtained window. It doesn't take long at all for the early autumn storm to rush through the streets of Wild Oak Woods, the scent of petrichor soon blotting out that of the Seelie fae.

I doze, my nose still as close to her scalp as I can make it, my heart a slow thud in my chest.

I wonder if she knows it beats for her now.

I wonder if maybe it always has.

CHAPTER TWENTY-SIX

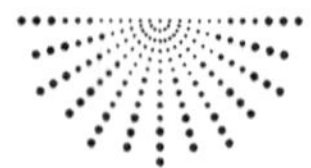

WREN

$\mathcal{I}$ am sore. *So* sore.

My brain clicks back on as soon as I open my eyes, the heavy weight draped over my body not Fenn or too many blankets.

No, it's Caelan. Caelan, who I had sex with… for literal hours.

Who says I'm his mate.

Who said he would ruin me for other men.

I'm not sure he's wrong about that last part.

I still don't know how I feel about the first part.

Rain pounds the window in my room, and I wonder if I would have more intense feelings about it either way if the light of day were present.

But right now, with him curled around me, cozy and snug under my sheets, rain slamming in sheets against the roof, I don't know if I care.

This feels right.

He feels right, like he was meant to be in my life. His cockiness and snark and even that self-satisfied smirk all feel like something that I've been missing.

Not to mention his actual cock. Who knew fae knotted?

Half the shifter romance books I read have knotting in them, and I always wondered if there was some truth to them knotting, but the fae?

A revelation.

A spiritual experience.

An *epiphany*.

The thought of being tied to Caelan, forever like he said, is jarring, though. Unexpected, and shocking, and altogether too new an idea to truly absorb.

I have time, though.

We have time.

I might not have whatever biological imperative is driving him, but I know I enjoy his company, and I enjoy what we did last night, and I'm very much enjoying being held just like this, on this rainy day.

A yawn stretches my jaw, and I stretch my legs out long, not wanting to disturb Caelan but too sore to not try to ease the ache.

"Good morning, lovely Wren," he murmurs in my ear. "You're hurting?"

The question is so sensitive, so unexpected, that emotion claws at my throat, raw and unbidden.

"Let me fix it." He doesn't wait for my answer, and as tight as my throat is, I'm not sure I could give him one anyway.

He swings me into his arms, standing gracefully in one smooth motion. "Bathroom?" he asks, and I nod, pleased and sleepy.

A small snort breezes against my hair, tickling my nose.

"I was trying to ask where it was," he says, a smile curling his lips. His light blue eyes are still sleepy, his usually perfectly coiffed hair mussed from my pillows, and he's never looked more charming and sweet.

"Oh," I say on a laugh. "It's through that door." I point.

He takes a few steps and opens it, only to sigh.

My closet stares back at him, and I can't help the laugh that bubbles in my chest.

"You think you're so funny, don't you?" His fingers tickle my ribs, and I squeal.

"I know I am," I finally wheeze when he stops.

His shoulders shake with laughter, and I lean my cheek against his chest, loving the sound of it, delighted that I'm the one who caused it.

Grumbling to himself, he chooses the correct door and steps into my bathroom.

My favorite space in the tiny apartment over my shop, and one I spent an inordinate amount of time getting exactly how I wanted it.

Navy-blue tiles are interspersed with white, from the floor to the walls and the ceiling. It took me hours of hyper-focused puzzling to suss out the exact pattern I would need to create a ceramic mural of stars and sky.

His jaw drops the moment he walks in, stopping at the threshold to admire my handiwork.

I try to see it through his eyes. Matte brass handles on the gnomish water pumps, something that cost me a pretty penny and set me back a good third of the inventory I inherited along with the store.

"I hemmed and hawed over the expense," I tell him, slightly shy about the extravagance of this space compared to every-thing else. "Then I decided that if I couldn't take care of my hands and back, I wouldn't be worth much as a jeweler for long."

"You designed this."

It's not a question, and I blush at the sheer admiration and wonder in his pronouncement.

"I like to bathe," I say sheepishly. "I wanted a space that was…

fully mine. It's probably silly because I should renovate the store too, but this… I need it." I shrug.

"You," he kisses my forehead, "are," he kisses one cheek, "a marvel." With that, he sets me in the hammered copper tub, and then stares at the faucets and knobs. "A marvel," he repeats.

"The gnomes did that," I tell him, folding my knees into my chest and reaching for the hot water lever. "I didn't have anything to do with the engineering."

The water gushes out of the tap, immediately filling the tub with a cloud of warm steam. When the water hits my hips, I wince.

"Poor little witch," Caelan murmurs. "Used and abused by her mate."

"Abused is taking it a bit far," I say, quirking an eyebrow. There's a little flurry of butterflies in my stomach at the word mate. "Don't think you were the only one who wanted it."

"Oh, don't worry, golden Wren, I won't be forgetting the way you begged for my knot, for me to come inside you, anytime soon. That's the stuff fantasies are made of."

I lock eyes with him, my nipples pebbling into hard peaks in spite of the hot water and steam.

"You know," he continues, his pupils dilating. "I think I should kiss it better, maybe."

My legs tighten reflexively and I clench around nothing, then wince again because hot damn, that hurt.

"Or I could just get you cleaned up." His eyes drop to the bottom of the tub, and I follow his gaze.

"Oh."

His spend leaks out of me, and he gives me a fully lascivious look before splashing as much as he can down the drain.

"I fucking love the way you look with my cum dripping out of your pretty pink cunt," he growls, nipping at my ear. Despite the soreness, I shiver, wondering how bad it would be if we did have sex again.

Worth it, most likely.

"Look how your body responds to me already," he says, smirking, plucking at one nipple.

I moan, arching into his touch, but he just laughs and gives me a devilish look.

One I like very, very much.

"Let me clean you up, sweet Wren," he soothes, and I nudge the drain shut, too tired and sore to argue with him.

Why would I? Getting pampered by Caelan sounds fantastic, thank you very much.

He opens the wooden armoire set against the wall, locating a fresh washcloth and soap as I lean against the back of the tub, eyes half-closed.

Grapefruit and rosemary fill the air as he lathers up the washcloth, taking pains to gently pull my hair out of the way as he massages my sore body slowly.

The knots and kinks built up from years of hunching over my jeweler's bench dissolve under his careful touch, and I hiss as he works at an especially painful spot under my shoulder blade.

"You know, you really ought to take better care of yourself," he says mildly, his fingers still kneading the spot. "Good thing you have me to do so now. You'd fall apart in a few more years."

I open my mouth to object to his censure, but he kisses the back of my neck and a shiver of pleasure renders me quiet.

The hot water's past my navel now, and I drowse as he rubs the washcloth all over my body, not missing a single bit of skin and paying special attention to all the tight muscles in my hands and wrists.

"Stand up," he commands, holding my waist as I sleepily do as he says. "I do like how quickly you did that," he says, brushing his mouth over a freshly cleaned hip before he bites it playfully.

I moan, my knees going weak, my body already ready for him again.

"Such a compliant, good little witch," he says, and I go hot all over at the praise.

He runs his fingers down my thigh, the washcloth following, and I relax under his ministrations again, telling myself I have too much to do today to spend it knotted in bed with him, no matter how tempting the idea.

No matter how much my body loves the idea of it.

No, I need to pinpoint the location of the dragon sapphire. I have gems and metal shavings and even herbs to inventory still. I have a few pieces I'd like to add to my store in the next month.

And I need to plan something masterful for the dragon sapphires once we beat the dwarves to them.

"Your forehead's creased," he mutters, running the washcloth over my calves. My skin is warm and slick with soap, and it glides effortlessly. "What is going on in that lovely head of yours, Wren?"

"Just thinking," I tell him.

"Then I'm not taking my job seriously enough."

"What do you—" I screech, a totally unsexy sound, as he catches me around the waist and throws my soaped up leg over one shoulder.

His hand finds my sex, and the noise abruptly turns into a groan as he glides his soapy hand between my folds, finding my clit with precise, gentle movements.

"You didn't think I was going to forget about cleaning this, did you?"

My breath hiccups as he pours a stream of hot water over it, rinsing the suds from my swollen pussy.

"Oh, you like that, don't you?" he grins up at me, then blows cold air across it.

I moan, my hands scrabbling at his shoulders.

"Please," I force out, needing release again, needing him to bring me to it, already a glutton for the pleasure I know he'll give me. "I want it." I squirm, my hips rising as he softly pets me, not enough to do anything but tease. "I need more."

"No, my love, I won't be knotting you again today," he laughs, and I suck in a breath as his fingernails bite into my ass, pulling me closer.

I'd be afraid of slipping were it not for the fact he's holding me up completely, my leg on his shoulder where he kneels on the other side of the tub, his hands gripping me tightly.

Then he licks, his hot tongue searing a path between my thighs, and any fear my mind's holding on to quickly vanishes as I rock forward.

"So fucking beautiful," he growls. His fingers find a rhythm as he massages my ass, leaving me limp and panting as he licks, and licks.

Pleasure begins to build immediately, and I whine. "I want you inside me," I say.

"No." He laughs again, his mouth still on me, and I rub myself against his mouth, shameless and needy. "I'll make you come like this, don't worry, love. You'll come all over my mouth again like the good little mate you are."

That word again.

It should scare me. I know it should, but right now, with his lips tight against my clit, his tongue working every nerve ending that matters, it just brings that orgasm within reach.

"So fucking good," he says, the words vibrating right where I need them.

"So close, so close," I pant.

He redoubles his efforts, licking and sucking and teasing me.

"More," I sob, the orgasm just out of reach, my body tired and reluctant after last night's marathon session of lovemaking.

"Oh, you want more, you greedy creature?" he glances up at me, his mouth glistening with my moisture, and I nod, desperate and just as greedy as he accuses me of being.

My eyes go wide, my jaw dropping, as his pinky finger finds its way to the tight hole of my ass, teasing at first.

"You wanted more," he says, shrugging under my leg. His chest muscles ripple, and I nod in encouragement. "I will give you whatever you need, Wren. Take your pleasure."

I moan again, the noise loud and wanton and completely without shame.

His finger slips inside me and he sucks—hard—at the same time.

Something incomprehensible and high-pitched comes out of my mouth and I slump over him, my orgasm shallower than last night but leaving me breathless all the same.

"I fucking love the way you look when you come," he purrs, carefully setting me back down in the tub.

I make a strangled noise as the hot water hits my crotch, and he laughs lightly.

"Did I kiss it better?" he asks, so smug.

I grin up at him sleepily, relaxed all over again. "I don't know. You could always try again later."

He throws back his head and laughs, the tips of his purple ears poking out from his dark hair, and I can't help but laugh along with him.

CHAPTER TWENTY-SEVEN

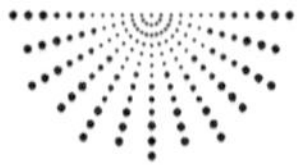

CAELAN

I like taking care of my Wren. My mate.

I even like the way she looks shocked and pleased every time I call her that, and though I want to press her on it, make her admit she's mine, I don't.

I don't want to push her away even more than I need her to tell me she accepts my claim.

If I do things right, which I will, all I have to do is be patient.

She's already blossomed like a fall rose under my care this morning. Her cheeks are flushed from the last orgasm I pushed her to, her skin soft and clean. I loved every minute of rubbing the delicately scented oil into her warm flesh after her bath.

I loved licking her until she shuddered and collapsed over me, and if I thought I was obsessed with her before, it has nothing on how I feel after knotting her.

I can be patient.

I wouldn't have made it centuries in the Underhill if I couldn't be.

She's curled by the fire, her sea-blue eyes rolling over page after page in the leather-bound geology book she seems to think will tell her exactly where her dragon sapphires are.

The rain's still coming down hard outside, her familiar Fenn appearing late this morning wet and put-out after being out in the storm. The cobblestone streets beneath her snug apartment are flooded, a river of water replacing the population of Wild Oak Woods.

Her store is closed as a result, as are most of the stores, everyone with good sense staying home.

The soup I'm making is one I remember my mother teaching me centuries ago, full of rich broth and tender meat and nutritious vegetables.

With any luck, it will help heal the sore places on Wren's feet, as well as any lingering pain from our night together.

My cock beads with moisture at the mere memory.

"Do you want to try looking for the sapphires again tomorrow?" I ask her, gritting my teeth and trying to get my aching cock to stand down.

The thought of cave delving should do the trick.

Unfortunately, the only cave I can think about delving is hers, and my cock grows even harder.

"I would like to find them as soon as I can." Her voice is faraway, her focus homed in on the book in her hands.

Fenn sits at my feet, his tail slapping against the floor, and, sighing, I dip the ladle into the stew and fish a piece of meat out for him.

He chirps happily, slurping it off the floor.

If I thought it smelled like wet dog when the Seelie brownie was here, it has nothing on the fox musk her familiar's emitting.

I'll have to figure out a way to fix that.

"Do you think it will continue to storm for long?" The question's mild, but my emotions are anything but.

I would very much like to stay with this woman for the next month while it rains.

Alas, I fear a monsoon is too much to wish for.

"It will probably let up tonight," she says. Her arms stretch overhead, and she points her bare feet.

Delighted, I watch her body shift under her loose dress, only to frown as my cock nudges against my pants.

"I should go inventory," she says glumly, snapping the book shut. "I'm not getting anywhere with this."

"The bread I made should be ready any second." It won't be as good as the baker witch next door's, but I've met very few creatures who could pass up bread fresh from the oven.

I don't want her to inventory. I don't want her hunched over her jewelry bench, or designing something to enchant with the dragon sapphires.

I want her naked and in my lap. I want to play with her while she comes over and over again, until she's addicted to my touch.

"Thank you for cooking." She licks her lips. "You didn't have to do that."

"I wanted to." Such a strange thing for her to say. "Why wouldn't I cook for us? For you?"

Her face turns slightly strange, and I peer at her. "What are you thinking about now?"

"Are you sure it isn't the binding spell?" Her white teeth pull at her bottom lip, turning it bright red, and I swallow a laugh.

I don't think she would take kindly to me laughing at her suggestion, even though it is patently absurd. "The binding spell?" I repeat, just to make sure I've heard her correctly.

She nods, her lower lip trembling slightly.

Carefully, I set the ladle on the plate I'm using for a rest and step over where Fenn has stretched across her floor. It takes me no time at all to take her chin in hand, her eyes wide and fearful.

"It's not the binding spell, you lovely fool. I don't know what I have to do to prove it to you." I chuckle, the sound low and dangerous. Simply the thought of not truly being her mate disgusts me. "I accepted the binding spell because I wanted to be close to you. I could have broken your colorful circle if I wanted to. I chose not to. I chose you."

"But—"

I stop whatever nonsense is about to come out of her mouth by planting mine on hers, claiming it. She tastes sweet as always, addictive and light against my tongue.

Making myself draw away, my gaze darts between her eyes until I laugh at her furrowed brow, rubbing it smooth with a finger.

"I can see you don't believe me still," I tell her, my ego slightly bruised but not surprised. "I'll just have to prove it to you."

Would that I could knot her again, take her right here, ass up on this chair in front of her fire, proving it to her with my flesh.

Wren is still too sore though, and knotting her again so soon is out of the question.

"Tell me what you've discovered about your sapphires, and I will try to figure out how to best help you find them."

She sighs, launching into an explanation of the cave systems around the Ever Forest and Wild Oak Woods. The longer she talks, hypothesizing about what she's read might mean, the more animated she grows.

Every word, every expression, is a gift, her trust in me hardly earned and completely shocking and endearing.

Oh, I think I will win the heart of my little witch, sooner or later.

CHAPTER TWENTY-EIGHT

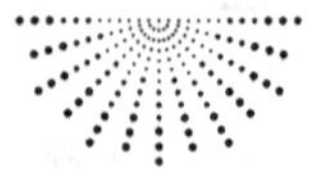

WREN

The rain finally lets up two days later. Sun streams through my windows, and Caelan left hours ago, apologizing profusely, promising to see me later, explaining he had to check on his friends and check in with Druze and Lila at Long Leaf Brews.

He was genuinely distraught, kissing me over and over again, as I assured him I understood.

Two whole days living in a blissful, snug domestic bubble with Caelan. He insisted on making every meal, massaging me, and giving me orgasms whenever I wanted.

I can't complain.

I do, however, wonder at the binding spell I cast. It gnaws at me, the knowledge that maybe I did something to cause him to become so attached to me prickling under my skin like a splinter I can't quite get rid of.

Caelan insists I'm wrong, but if I botched the spell and did this to him, I need to know.

At the same time, I don't want to know.

I hope I am wrong.

I've gotten accustomed to the idea of him being around. I like his quick wit, his cocky smirks, and the way he takes care of me.

He's a great cook, a generous lover, and has all the makings of a great partner, Unseelie fae or not.

I care about him. Which feels silly, feels too soon, like maybe I'm just naïve and wishful instead of truly thinking about the reality of what it would mean if I were actually his mate.

My parents had a happy marriage, a normal marriage, no mates at all, and though it was clear every day that they loved and respected each other, they made sure to tell me often that relationships, no matter your partner, were like a living thing.

My mom often compared their marriage to taking care of a plant—it required thought, and water and sunshine and fertilizer. It was work, but a job they were both proud to contribute to, and as a result, I got to see what a healthy marriage looked like: a partnership, full of love and respect.

Not that I've had an inclination or opportunity to even try to find the same thing.

No, I've been so preoccupied with my ejection from my coven, then my rejection from the guild, that I have hardly made time for anything but leveling up my spellcasting and refining my craftsmanship.

When it comes to Caelan… I don't know what to think.

All I know for sure, though, is that I already care about him, and we seem to work really well together. It's easy with him, and I can't believe my good luck.

Yet the idea nags at me that maybe the stupid spell I cast could be influencing him, or have backfired on his Unseelie fae blood, seeing as how he's not the demon the spell was built for…

My stomach turns.

It doesn't matter how much he insists otherwise, the possibility remains.

At least he left—if he was still hanging around here and doting on me, I would be even more suspicious.

Stupidly, I already miss him. I keep opening my mouth to tell him something funny I just thought of only to realize he's not there.

Talking to Fenn isn't quite the same.

The fox glances up at me as I think of him, and I reach down to scratch the soft fur behind his pointed ears.

"I'm ridiculously behind on everything," I tell him, and his ears twitch, his long-lashed eyes soft and warm as he rubs his face against my ankle. "I haven't gotten any closer to finding the dragon sapphires, I haven't done anything to show the guild they need me, and all I've managed to do is sleep, eat, have sex, and read this book for the club tonight." I pick up the book in question, a romance about a human knight and a mermaid who makes a deal with a witch to give him a merman's tail but forgets to ensure he can breathe underwater.

Another example of witches being ostracized in literature, despite the fact the witch in question was likely overwhelmed with work from the locals and the mermaid could have been more particular in her request.

"But noooo, somehow it's all the witch's fault!" I tell Fenn, glaring at the linen-bound novel. Sighing, I pick it up and put it in my leather pack. The sun's setting on Wild Oak Woods, I have made absolutely no money in the last few days, thanks to the relentless rain and flooded streets, and now I have to go be social at a book club about a book in which the witch is the villain.

Not to mention I miss Caelan.

Grumpy, I run the brownie's gifted comb through my hair one last time before throwing my hands up and deciding it's good enough.

Fenn trots behind me as I make my way out of the shop's front exit, carefully locking up everything as I did before.

Thankfully, several days of sitting around with Caelan—my

cheeks go fiery as I realize maybe sitting around isn't the best descriptor of the past few days—means my heels have healed, though the rest of me is quite sore from all our… activity.

The thought of him sends heat through my body, soothing the ache he's caused.

I take a deep breath, inhaling the crisp scent of cooler weather on the horizon, a sure sign summer's truly fading into autumn.

By the time I make it to The Listening Page bookstore, I'm in a noticeably better mood, the fading sunshine and breeze doing wonders for my introverted bad attitude after being cooped up for a few days, even with Caelan's inimitable company.

The door to Ruby's shop's propped open with a large brass planter, a green patina of verdigris snaking charmingly up the side of it. Small pink roses and purple pansies spill over the side, perfuming the air. Fenn even stands up on his hind feet, his little nose twitching as he sniffs the flowers.

"Spelled," I tell him, and he yips in agreement. What charm's been worked on the planter, I'm not sure, but judging from the way my entire body relaxes as I enter the store, I have a guess or two.

And I'm certainly not about to complain about it.

A neat piece of spellwork, one I should probably employ at my own shop door.

Still, a faint tingle of nervousness grips me as I walk through the door. Unlike the last time I was here, the store is full of chattering voices, drowning out the sound of the crackling fire.

Ruby's cat yowls, jumping down from a high bookshelf near the door and flouncing around Fenn, with eyes the size of dinner plates.

Fenn must pass inspection because the fluffy cat saunters off without incident, and I let out a shaky breath as I shove my shoulders back and head toward the sound of conversation.

"You made it!" Ruby claps her hands as I round the corner.

At least two dozen mismatched chairs are arranged in a semicircle around the massive stone hearth, and an impeccably arranged table flows down the length of it. Cheeses and breads and pastries and dried sausages and fruit slices form artful pinwheels and flowers, and I take it in for a beat, hungry after the past few days' exertion.

"I'm so glad you're here," a familiar voice says, and I finally look up from the impressive spread.

To my surprise, I recognize nearly all the readers in attendance. A smile tugs up the corner of my lips, and for a split second, I wonder why I was so anxious about coming to the book club.

Ruby, of course, I met the other day, but Piper's also there, waving at me from a deep teal velvet chair that looks like she might disappear if she sits too deeply in it.

Nerissa's thumbing through her copy of the book on the fireplace hearth, her legs tucked underneath her as she scowls at the pages, her face nearly hidden behind her dark hair. A blonde elf's ears peek out from a crown of complicated braids—I'm fairly certain that's Lila from Caelan's tea shop, and I make a mental note to go pick up some tea from her. Rosalina's in deep conversation with Willow, her mouse familiar washing his face with careful pink paws.

There are plenty of faces that are new to me too, a satyress with delicately feathered hooves peeking out from a long floral dress, another elfin woman whose face I recognize but whose name I can't remember, and a green-skinned and emerald-haired woman who I'd bet money is a dryad.

There is only a pair of men amongst all the women, and they share a kiss before one feeds another a piece of jam-topped cookie.

It's a good vibe.

"The food looks too pretty to eat," I tell Ruby, barely managing to catch Fenn as he leaps into my arms. He yips at me, and Ruby lets out a low laugh, her eyebrows raised.

"You should probably give him some sausage before he starts Maximillian to howling." She jerks her chin at the fireplace, where the great big fluffy cat sits, his eyes glowing in the light from the fire, tail twitching at his side.

"Is he your familiar?" I ask, though I'm fairly certain that's exactly what he is.

"Familiar is probably the nice way to put it." Ruby laughs again, the sound so contagious I smile. "He'd probably say I'm his servant if he could talk. Grab some snacks, pull up a chair, and we'll be getting started in just a moment." She pauses, her lips pursing, and then she nods to herself. "I thought maybe we could… the witches, I mean, have a chat afterwards, that is, if you don't have plans." The words tumble out of her mouth, and she wrings her hands together.

I recognize the nervous gesture all too well. "Sure, of course I can stay."

She lets out a long sigh, her shoulders sagging slightly. "Good, that's good." She beams at me, ushering me over to the table.

Piper stands up, her deer familiar snoozing on the floor beside her, barely moving as Piper steps over her velvety hindquarters, making a beeline for me.

"What is on your neck?" she asks, her brown eyes round. Her hand drifts towards my right ear, and I slap it away on reflex.

Piper's mouth goes round, and then she covers it with a hand. "No," she says on an exhale.

"It's a bruise." I pull my hair over it, slightly embarrassed. Why is it that I have to blush at everything? Why can't I just have the complexion where nothing ever turns me red?

"It's a hickey," she hisses, grabbing my hair before I have a chance to stop her, peeking under it and then smiling in triumph. "A good one, too."

"I think I fucked up," I admit, covering my face as I whisper.

"What? Because someone kissed you so much they left a little love mark right there?" She's gleeful, doing a funny little step-dance around me.

"No," I say, trying to flee from her perusal as I make my way to the table laden with cheese and sausage and fruit and yummy-looking pastries. I don't even bother with a plate, suddenly totally overwhelmed at the reality of what I might have done to Caelan to make him give me that bruise.

"Then what?" Her expression changes. "Did somebody hurt you? I'll hex them so they can't shit for a year," she says, and there's no chance she doesn't mean it.

"It was Caelan," I say around the cheese, then toss a piece of sausage to where Fenn's patiently waiting. He snatches it out of the air, then disappears under an empty chair to enjoy his treat.

"So?" and then— "Oh. Ooooh." She looks scandalized, her eyebrows disappearing into her chocolatey brown hair. "You made him kiss you?"

"No, I didn't make him kiss me," I wail. "I'm afraid it was a reaction to the binding."

The conversation all around us dies, and I realize I've practically screamed my problem to the entire reading circle.

Oh, fuck. *Fuck!*

Lila's staring at me, her brow wrinkled in concern, a piece of sausage paused halfway to her mouth.

Nerissa's looked up from the mermaid/knight romance, her head tilted to the side as she considers what I've just yelled at everyone.

"Impossible," Nerissa says smoothly, not even bothering to look up from her book.

Piper puts a firm hand on the small of my back and pushes me to the hearth, where I plop down. My handful of smoked cheese stares up at me forlornly, and I promptly stuff it into my gob, chewing as I attempt to calm my stampeding heart.

And attempt to avoid saying anything else stupid.

"You think the binding went wrong," Piper murmurs, her face completely serious, eyebrows cinched together.

"Impossible," Nerissa repeats, this time glancing up at me.

She sighs as she inspects my face and sets her book down on the stones.

"Why do you think something backfired?" Piper presses.

"Because… because…" I trip over the word. How am I supposed to tell them that he said I'm his mate? That he… knotted me?

My face turns beet-red and I shove the rest of the cheese into my mouth and cover my face with my hands.

"Oooooh," Nerissa says in a low, knowing voice. "No wonder he didn't try to break the binding or resist at all."

I glance sidelong at her and she nods at me, a faint smile kicking up the sides of her mouth.

"You're his mate," she finally pronounces.

The silence is deafening, and I just shrug.

"They *mate?*" Piper asks.

I peek at her through my fingers, and she peels my hands from my face.

"They do." Nerissa sounds positively gleeful. "And Caelan's must be Wren."

"But what if it's my fault and he just thinks I am? What if I messed up? What if everything he's saying and doing is just some stupid mistake I made?"

Ruby plops down in front of me, her wide, window-pane-print trousers puddling around her legs. She pushes up her glasses. "The fae mating bond can't be faked."

"Exactly," Nerissa agrees.

"It's primal," Ruby adds primly.

I look up as a loud conversation breaks out again, all around me.

Everyone here has been listening in on my mental break-down, but they're not whispering behind their hands about me, like they would have in my old coven. They're not staring at me with horrified expressions.

No, they look truly concerned, each piping up with their own stories about the Unseelie fae, about mates, and about binding spells. Well, nearly everyone, the satyress just nods sagely at the various pieces of advice floating around.

"Caelan has a hard shell around him," Lila advises, a soft smile on her lips. "But he has a good heart, no matter how hard he tries to hide it. Sure, he can be short-tempered, but some of our guests even annoy Druze, and he's hard to ruffle. He's a good male, Wren."

"Binding spells should be easy for the fae to break. I was half-expecting him to easily unwind our spell that night."

"See?" Piper says, gesturing to everyone. "This is not the end of the world."

"But we ate your sexy cookie, Piper," I moan. "What if it interacted with it? It was much, much stronger than it should have been. It was less of an alluring charm and more of an immediately jump your bones charm."

Her nose wrinkles. "That was a stronger batch than I intended, but it wouldn't have pushed you that far. And it shouldn't have worked on a fae at all."

"Yeah, those cookies are delicious but they don't work on me," Lila agrees.

"That's what he said, but what if—"

"Nope," Ruby shakes her head, and Piper grins at her. "We're not going to support your catastrophizing, are we, team?"

"I mean, I like drama as much as the next person," one of the men chimes in, "but I think you're looking for a reason to run. And trust me, I am one to know."

"He really is," his partner agrees, squeezing his hand. "It took me years to lock him down. If you like this fae and he's committed to you, what reason is there to run?"

"The fear of ruining it all," the other guy says, rolling his eyes. "Obviously."

"Obviously!" I agree, pointing at him because he gets it.

Oh.

Everyone's peering at me with what would be comical, matching expressions in various degrees of 'I told you so.'

"Oh," I say out loud. "Okay. Oookay."

"Okay," Piper says, clapping her hands. "Well. That's that problem solved. You like him, he's obsessed with you—"

"Lucky," Willow mutters, so low I'm not sure I heard her right.

"And now we can talk about the book," Ruby concludes.

Fenn darts out from under the chair, sniffing my hand before tugging at my trousers, leading me over to the table for more food.

This time, I grab a plate like I have a modicum of manners, but when I sit down in one of the mismatched, warm chairs by the fire, I can't concentrate on the conversation about the mermaid and the knight.

All I can think is maybe, just maybe, Caelan really does care about me.

CHAPTER TWENTY-NINE

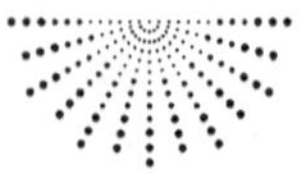

CAELAN

The Rowdy Wolf Tavern hardly lives up to its name.

Other than a group of respectfully loud minotaurs, the atmosphere, while jovial, would be best described as calming.

Dark, polished wood paneling and low lighting set the tone for conversation, the drinks surprisingly good, though they don't have the fae brews we're all used to.

Ga'Rek guzzles from a stone stein. The shifter female who owns the tavern took one look at him when we walked in and pulled out a vessel that looked to be carved from granite.

"Good stuff," he says. The table shakes where he sets it down, and he wipes the back of his hand over his mouth.

I grin at him, amused as always by how orcish he is, despite me stealing him away from his parents at such a young, impressionable age.

The way they treated him, though… he's always said I did him a favor getting him out of there.

"Why are you smiling like that?" Ga'Rek asks, tilting his head at me, his tusks gleaming in the low light.

"Like what?" I ask.

Kieran's watching me from the darkened corner of our table, his wings, for once, blessedly silent under the green carapace shielding them. He's taken to wearing a charcoal-grey wool cloak since our first day here, presumably to avoid undue attention.

His attitude, at least, is somewhat less sulky than usual.

"Why aren't you asking Kieran why he hasn't found something to complain about?"

"No, you're not getting off that easy. Where in the name of the moon have you been the last few days?" The table groans as the huge orc sets his arms down on it, leaning forward to inspect my face. "We were fucking worried about you, Caelan."

"Worried?" I huff a laugh, raising an eyebrow. "About me? Why?"

"Because my mother wants us all dead, you ass," Kieran mutters. "We thought you'd either been caught or defected back to her."

The very idea puts my hackles up. "I would never go back, not now that I've found—"

"Ah-HA!" Ga'Rek shouts, causing the nearby patrons to look over at us. The chandelier overhead, lit by the same magic flowers as the street lanterns, swings slightly from the force of his voice. "I knew it. I knew it."

"Knew what?" I school my expression into one of pure innocence, but Ga'Rek claps me on the back, causing me to cough. "The fact you're able to work in that pastry shop without wrecking the entire kitchen is a miracle."

He glares at me, but as always, his ire is short-lived, and his frown immediately perks back up into a smile. He sits back in his chair, stretching an arm over the back of the empty one next to him.

The table's structural integrity doesn't seem to be too

adversely affected by him, but I glance at the legs of it, just in case.

"The damned tattoo on your arm." He reaches out and grabs my sleeve, tugging it up.

He's damnably fast for his size, and even though I could probably stop him, I let him.

"What in the…" Kieran leans forward, his eyes huge in his face, his wings buzzing, the cloak on his shoulders moving strangely as he grows excited. "I thought that was a myth. Who?"

"Only the most beautiful witch," I start, but Ga'Rek's face turns stricken and I pause, tilting my head in confusion.

"Not Willow," Kieran rasps. "You've hardly ever seen her, it can't be Willow, she cannot be your mate—"

"Wren," I interrupt his tirade before it begins. Both males sit back in their chairs, their faces going blank before they both smile broadly at me.

Interesting.

"So, you are attracted to Willow, are you?" I ask, giddy at a new piece of information on the young Unseelie noble.

"This isn't about Kieran," Ga'Rek all but roars, then raises his huge stein in the air. "A toast to Caelan and Wren. Fate has found you willing!"

Laughing, I clink my glass against his gently, hoping the brute doesn't shatter it in his excitement.

"When?" Kieran asks, none of his usual put-upon silence present now. No, his eyes practically sparkle, his wings beating a low-level hum inside their hard protective layer. "When did the mate marks appear?"

"As soon as Wren walked into the bakery," I say smugly. "The very first day."

Kieran blows out a breath, then takes a long swallow from his drink, then another, and another, until there's none left.

"I knew it," Ga'Rek jeers, clearly thrilled on my behalf.

Kieran pushes his chair out and heads back to the bar top without a word.

We both watch him for a moment.

"He was worried for you," Ga'Rek finally says, breaking the silence between us. "I've never seen him like that. Worried about someone besides himself, I mean." He narrows his eyes at me. "I was worried too."

Something like guilt rears its head in my chest, and I take a long drink as I grapple with the odd, discomfiting sensation.

"He thought his mother had found you. He was beside himself. Tried not to show it, you know, but his—"

"Wings gave him away," I finish for him. I wince as Ga'Rek nods.

"You look uncomfortable," Ga'Rek says cheerfully, grinning broadly at me from over his stone stein.

I grumble something under my breath.

"What's that, old friend?" Ga'Rek asks merrily.

"I said I shouldn't have left without an explanation." I rake hand through my hair, then retie the leather thong around the length of it.

Ga'Rek whistles low.

Kieran plops back into the chair, his drink slopping over the side of the cup. "What's all that about?" he asks, not sounding at all like himself.

The thought of him worried about me warms a part of my heart I didn't know I still possessed.

I clear my throat, the words sticking in it.

Ga'Rek narrows his eyes at me, smiling even wider.

The asshole.

I cough, then blurt— "I'm sorry I left and you were worried."

Kieran blinks in surprise, then his royal training takes over and he bows his head, accepting the coughed out apology without another word from me.

"I would have blamed myself forever if she'd taken you," he says in a gravelly voice.

Two things hit me full force, then; one, that the sulking prince has a hidden depth. And two, how much it means to me to have these two friends at my side.

My eyes sting, probably from the smokey interior.

"We need to meet Wren," Ga'Rek says, looking between the two of us Unseelie with what appears to be a suppressed laugh.

I glare at him. "Why?"

"Because if she's mated to our oldest and best friend, we need to warn her what she'll be in for."

Kieran laughs, a low, bell-like tone full of rippling power. The hairs on the back of my neck stand up, and Ga'Rek and I share a surprised look.

Kieran doesn't seem to notice, simply drinking deeply from his refilled cup.

"What's she like?" Ga'Rek asks.

"She's…" I shake my head. The vines of the mate mark curl up my wrist and I roll my shirtsleeves up, taking a long look at it. "She's clever, and talented, and beautiful. I don't know what I did to deserve her, but I want to prove I'm worthy of every second I spend in her presence."

Ga'Rek claps his hands together. "Making an honest male out of you. I like her already. Can't say I would believe it if I wasn't seeing it with my own eyes."

I frown. "I'll never be honest."

"Sure you won't," Ga'Rek says. He raises his hand again to smack me on the back, but I swat it away. He leans forward. "You know she's Piper's best friend, right?"

"I figured they were close."

"Piper will be upset if you do anything to hurt her."

I bristle, my fangs lengthening. "Don't even suggest it," I hiss, my voice dangerous.

Ga'Rek raises his hands in surrender. "I wasn't. I was simply stating the obvious. And if you are so set on staying a trickster, then…"

"We aren't in the Underhill anymore," Kieran interrupts, his eyes glistening. He unbuckles the cloak from around his shoulders, tossing it over the back of his chair. His beetle wings buzz for a moment, then swing free of the hard shell. He cracks his neck, one shoulder rolling as though the wings, or more likely, the task of keeping them put away, has bothered him.

"We can be whatever we want to be. What is a prince without a throne? And Caelan doesn't have to be a trickster. By the moon, you're hardly a warrior now, Ga'Rek, you're a damned pastry chef." Kieran slaps a hand on the table, his wings vibrating slightly behind him, the light dancing off the shining membrane and reflecting off the walls. "Is this what we'll be forever? Me working in a greenhouse and apothecary, you filling eclairs—"

Ga'Rek clears his throat, turning a deeper shade of green that I know means he's embarrassed.

"And you, Caelan, serving tea to dwarves and minotaurs and the other riff-raff?" His voice has gotten loud. "Is this all we have? Serving at the behest of a group of covenless witches?"

"That's my mate you're talking about," I snarl, half-standing.

"Oy there," the female shifter behind the bar chucks a dirty rag at Kieran and it makes a wet sound as it plops against one of his glistening wings.

The fae prince sucks in a breath, flushing maroon in fury.

"Don't fucking start, Kieran," I warn him.

"Don't worry, I'm done." With that, the fallen prince stands, drawing up to his full height, power settling on him like a mantle.

The bar goes quiet, even the duo playing the fiddle on a makeshift stage breaking off their song.

Kieran takes one last conceited look around, then stomps out of the tavern without another word, the door slamming behind him.

"He's not taking it well," Ga'Rek observes as conversation

reaches a normal pitch again, the musicians starting back up with a jaunty tune. "But he has a point. Is this what we want to do?"

"Lila and Druze are good people," I say, turning it over. "Do you dislike working for Piper?"

The orc flushes again, running the tip of his tongue down one fang. "No." A short, terse syllable that doesn't leave a lot of room for supposition.

And yet. And yet… I wonder at him. The orc, who I've seen bathed in the blood of our enemies, a raging force on the battle-field, a berserker and a credit to his kind—now stuck in a hot kitchen for a flighty twit of a witch.

We sit in silence, each lost in our own thoughts, when it occurs to me.

What I want—that is, what I want *besides* Wren.

"Where are you going?" Ga'Rek asks, a laugh on his lips despite the edge to his voice. "Back to your witch already?"

"To see a man about an idea," I tell him, smirking, knowing keeping my plan secret from him will drive him crazy.

You can take a fae from the Underhill, but you can't take the trickster out of a fae.

CHAPTER THIRTY

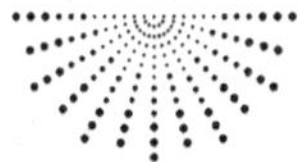

WREN

By the time the book discussion wraps up, the fire's nearly burned itself to embers in the hearth, the once-laden table now nearly bare of all the pastries and cheese and fruit.

Although I'm fairly certain the familiars helped lighten it, it's still impressive.

Despite the fact I've been distracted and blushing for the past three hours, not to mention sore even in the plush chair, I've enjoyed listening to everyone else talk.

It's shocking.

I've enjoyed being a part of this group, even if I was basically on the fringes of it, and warmth spreads across my chest at the knowledge.

There was no pretense, no snide comments or sneers. No mean whispers or pointed observations, not even one rude look.

It's so completely different than the groups I tried to fit in with in the city, especially in my old coven, that I'm not sure what to do with myself.

It's hard to believe it's even possible—that a group of so many different species from so many walks of life could get along in such a way, brought together to discuss this romance novel.

The satyress waves at me as she leaves, the human couple also calling out their farewells as the door to The Listening Page closes behind them.

A steady patter of rain begins to fall on the bookstore's windows, and the human men laugh as they run past, attempting to outrun the gathering storm.

"What did you think?" Ruby's standing in front of me, a wide smile on her face. She pushes her glasses up on her nose, clutching her copy of the book to her chest. Maximilian winds around her ankles. Fenn jumps on my lap, yipping at the cat, who simply gives him a baleful look until Fenn quiets, twitching.

"It was… perfect." I'm embarrassed to tell her I was so anxious about it, but I can't deny I'm relieved. So relieved. "Everyone was so nice."

"Not always," Nerissa chimes in, moving a platter out of the way to sit on the table. "They're not always nice."

"Who is?" Willow asks her tartly, flipping her auburn hair over her shoulder. "No one is always nice, Nerissa."

"I didn't mean anything by it," Nerissa snipes back.

I sigh, somewhat used to their bickering but annoyed all the same.

"Not everything is a question of the balance of light and dark," Nerissa continues, clearly ruffled, though about what, I have no idea.

"Enough," Piper thunders. The typically sugary-sweet Piper stands in front of the fire, her arms crossed over her chest, and despite her petite size, she radiates power.

Strength.

Nerissa and Willow fall quiet, sufficiently chastised.

Ruby claps her hands twice, and the five of us focus on her.

"It's high time Wild Oak Woods had a coven, don't you think?" Ruby asks, but there's no real question attached.

"I have the paperwork for us to get established. I had it drawn up a long time ago, actually…" She clears her throat, a strange expression on her face. "Now is the time, though."

"Now is the time," Nerissa agrees, nodding dramatically. "Change is coming."

"Change is here," Willow says, but she's not arguing. "It's time."

The four of them look at me, and I realize they're waiting for me to weigh in. I've been a part of this group for longer than I knew, and suddenly, I wonder at Caelan's claims to be servant to the whims of fate.

Certainly, this group, these women… this feels as meant to be as he and I.

"I agree. It's time."

My heart thrums in my chest as Piper pulls out the paperwork that will establish us as an official coven in the kingdom.

Willow's right. Change *is* here.

The question I keep coming back to, though, is what is driving it?

CHAPTER THIRTY-ONE

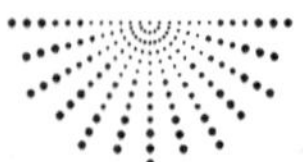

CAELAN

Hash Beauchamp's bright brown eyes find mine the moment I sit on the porch of his old inn in the rocking chair next to him.

Despite the fact the place is downtrodden and tired, and that Hash himself is about as curmudgeonly as a man can get, I've taken a liking to both the inn and him.

We rock in silence next to each other, the charmed flowers in the lanterns overhead casting a soft glow over the sagging porch. More flowers trail up the side of the porch railing, night-blooming buds releasing a spicy floral scent in the air.

"You seen my Boner?" Hash asks, and I can't keep the laugh from bubbling up.

"He's asleep on the step there," I say, pointing at the half-dead mutt.

"Mmph." Hash's rocking slows and he stops, bracing his skinny arms on his knees. "That's not why you sat out here next to me, is it? For me to talk about my sweet Boner."

"Can't say it is," I manage, unbelievably remaining straight-faced.

"What's on your mind then, Purple?"

Purple. It's what he's decided to call me, basically since the moment he set eyes on me. Not fairy, or wretch, or evil demon fae, or any of the other nicknames humans have called me over the centuries, but *Purple*.

The man's got a way with names, I suppose.

"How do you like running this place? The inn, I mean," I tack on, in case he's predisposed to talk about his Boner again. Which, as I know all too well, he *always* is.

"The inn? It's hard for an old man, to be honest with you." His white eyebrow, thick as a cave caterpillar, arches up as he studies me. The light plays across his craggy face. "You know, I've been meaning to find someone to take the old girl over."

It takes me a beat to realize the inn is the old girl. I hold my breath, waiting.

Boner stands up and barks once, then makes a slow, sad limp up the stairs.

Hash and I watch his progress, the music of the crickets providing a certain ambiance to the old dog's plop back down on the porch.

His tongue hangs out further than seems physically possible.

"Always makes me laugh to see Boner go limp like that," Hash says.

I squint at him. There's no way he doesn't know exactly what he's named his dog after.

"You interested?" he asks.

"In a limp Boner?"

He stares at me. I stare at him.

Hash bursts into laughter. "What the hell are you talking about? You fae crack me up, you know that, Purple?"

I grin at him, amused by his amusement.

"Alright, I tell you what. You drive a hard bargain, I know all about that with you Unseelie fellas, but I'll settle on it. You take care of my dog, and you take care of the old girl here, and I'll consider our debt even."

"What—" I half-stand, the rocking chair wobbling beneath me.

Boner opens one eye, his pink and black speckled tongue still lolling out.

"Don't say you never drove a hard bargain with a Seelie. I think my time here is up, though. I think it's time for a change in Wild Oak Woods."

There's no flash of light, no cloud of smoke, just a faint glimmer around Hash Beauchamp as the Seelie glamour falls away.

Hash reaches out, gripping my wrist with young, smooth-skinned fingers.

"She's yours, Caelan of the Underhill. The deed is in your room. Sign it, and the land and inn are yours, too. She's full of secrets, as is Wild Oak Woods. It's time for me to find a new adventure. Take care of Boner." The Seelie fae winks at me once, his laughter bell-like, so beautiful it sends a pang through my chest, and then he disappears.

Boner whines, then stretches long, clearly beyond caring that Hash Beauchamp was a Seelie fae this whole time, and beyond caring that I'm now supposed to take care of him.

"How about that," I say to myself quietly, sitting back in the rocking chair.

There will be strings attached to this place, there's no doubt about that.

I'm sure there was some magic I didn't notice tying me here as soon as I met that wily Hash. Distracted by Wren, and everything a mate could mean to me, I've certainly sealed my fate here at this ancient inn.

"Huh," I say again, scratching my jawline. The chair creaks as I rock.

It means something, I'm sure of it.

An Unseelie trickster fae hoodwinked by a golden fae from the Seelie Court.

This inn, old and in disrepair, practically falling down around me.

It means something. I just don't know what.

Boner lets out a massive fart, and I wrinkle my nose.

184

I lock the door behind me, climbing the stairs to my snug home over the store and mull it over.

The stairs creak as I walk, the sound comforting.

As comforting as the knowledge that I'm not on the outside, not anymore, that the group of us witches, the witches of Wild Oak Woods, have set something in motion.

Our coven will be the first in this small town on the edge of the Ever Forest, and there's something important about that, all on its own.

I'll be the first of something.

A founding member.

A part of something more, with a group of witches I truly like.

By the time I lock my front door, Fenn zooming around the apartment and yipping, I'm in a fantastic mood.

Maybe I've found a permanent place here in Wild Oak Woods, after all.

Maybe this… beautiful thing I've started with Caelan will last, too.

I take my time soaking in the tub, using a special blend of salts and lavender I bought from Willow to ease my sore muscles.

When I climb into the bed alone, I miss Caelan, but I don't feel alone.

Not anymore.

❧

"WHAT IS IT," I slur, clawing at my sleep-filled eyes.

The hammering noise continues, relentless, and I look around blearily before sliding out of my bed. It's still dark out, though the rosy fingers of dawn have started to stretch over the treetops in the distance.

Yawning, I stretch my arms high overhead before padding my way to the window. The patterned curtains are soft against my hands as I pull them back, peeking outside and expecting to see Caelan or smoke and a fire or something—but not Piper.

Piper, who's sobbing, holding a massive wicker basket covered in hot pink checkered fabric. Piper, who's knocking on my front door, making the bell overhead jingle with every strike.

I throw open the window, or try, before realizing I've never opened it and it's painted shut.

Ew. I should ask my brownie to fix that.

Grimacing, I toss my threadbare robe over myself and sprint downstairs. I nearly die when Fenn bounds out in front of me like a homicidal cat, but I manage to keep my balance in spite of him.

Finally, I fling open the door, and Piper howls in anguish when she sees me, flinging her arms around me.

The smell of sweet bread and jam waft from her basket and I hug her back, my stomach flip-flopping with worry... and then growling loudly.

"She, she—" Piper attempts. Her frantic tears soak the fabric of my flimsy robe and I pat her back, shushing her and slightly out of my element.

Okay, maybe completely out of my element. "What is it, Piper? Are you hurt?"

"She—she's coming for the autumn festival and, and—" she wails as a fresh bout of sobs rack her.

"I don't understand, Piper, come upstairs and I'll fix us some tea, and you can tell me all about it, okay?"

Piper makes a senseless noise that I assume is agreement, and I hurry her up the stairs before she can start sobbing again.

I take the basket from her and set it on the table, putting the kettle on for fresh ginger peach black tea, and cast her a worried look.

I've only known Piper for a handful of months now, but I've never seen her like this. The closest I've seen her to truly upset was when she couldn't get a specialty flavor right. Her hands twist in front of her at the table, shaking slightly.

The cabinet door creaks as I open it, digging through my cups to find the sturdiest one.

"Why is there a cup of milk on the table?" she asks, sniffling.

"I have a brownie, remember? That's what they like."

The tea kettle begins whistling, and I add the steaming water to the pot and take my time setting it on the table, putting an old crocheted doily under the pot. It's seen better days, slightly stained and frayed. I make a mental note to do better about keeping a few things company-ready.

It alarms me slightly to realize that I haven't had anyone over to my small apartment besides Caelan.

Not even Piper.

Some friend I am.

I pour a steady stream of hot tea into the sturdy ceramic mug, then pour myself a cup.

"Honey?" she asks, sniffling.

"Of course," I tell her. "I bought some the other day, it's from Willow's bees."

"W-w-willow makes the best hon-hon-honeeeeyyyyy." Her forehead thunks against the table, her shoulders shaking in despair.

Fenn puts his paws on the table, staring at the top of Piper's head in confusion, head tilted.

"Piper, tell me what's wrong or Fenn is going to start yowling, and trust me, you do not want that," I snap, my voice firmer than I meant.

Her shoulders still, and then she draws a shaking breath.

When she manages to sit up, Fenn yips at her, body completely stiff.

"The Duchess is coming, for the autumn f-f-f-festival," she sucks in a huge breath before continuing, fresh tears rolling down her ruddy cheeks.

"That's great," I say, my eyebrows rising. "That will be wonderful for the town, and hopefully bring us a lot of business and the opportunity to attract even more visitors—"

"Everything has to be perfect," she screams.

Fenn raises his head and I sigh, burying my face in my hands as he takes up the cry, howling.

A fox howl, to be clear, is not a normal dog howl. Or a cat howl.

No, it sounds like someone is torturing and murdering a human. That is the sound a fox makes.

Unpleasant doesn't begin to cover it.

Unpleasantly demonic would be a closer description.

The silver lining, however, is that it seems to shock Piper out of her sobbing, and she sits up, staring at Fenn, who keeps screaming.

And screaming.

"Thank you, Fenn, that will be enough," I tell him crisply.

He snaps his mouth shut and circles around the table, nosing his way into Piper's lap.

"I left Velvet at home in her bed," she says. "I couldn't bear to wake her." Her trembling hands stroke Fenn's soft fur, and I push her mug of steaming tea closer.

"Honey," I say vaguely, then jump up and grab the speckled pot from Willow and drop the dipper in. Golden honey streams into her steaming mug and she wraps her hands around it as I dunk the dipper back in the pot.

"Thank you." Another sniff. "There's pastries in the basket—"

"I thought you'd never offer," I say, ravenous as I flip over the pink-checked cloth and pull out a cheese Danish. "My favorite."

"It has a calming charm—"

I don't hear whatever else she's going to tell me because that's all I need to hear. I shove one in her mouth, and her brown eyes go wide as she sputters, then chews.

My eyes narrow as I watch her swallow, her throat bobbing, and the effect is nearly as immediate as Fenn's horrible howl.

"Oh," she says on a sigh, slumping back in the chair. "That's better. Why didn't I think of that?"

"Probably because you were really upset," I tell her. I grab a cheese Danish for myself, eyeing it before taking a bite. "The cookie really did a number on me, by the way."

"I told you," she says, wiping her nose with a floral embroidered napkin that the brownie must have left last night. "You had to have already been very attracted to the person for it to have that effect." A sly smile curves her lips.

I roll my eyes but smile back at her. "You got me there." On impulse, I reach across the table and squeeze her hand. "Tell me what's wrong, Piper. Help me understand. You're my friend. My best friend. I don't know how to help you unless you let me." The admission makes me feel vulnerable, but I know it's the right thing to say.

Until her eyes fill up with fresh tears, and I feel mine do the same.

"I thought you said these were charmed for calm," I choke out through a teary laugh.

"They are, but now I'm weepy because that was *sweet*."

I scoff but give her hand one last squeeze before topping off her mug of tea.

"Alright." She rolls her neck, then puts her shoulders back and looks me square in the eye. "The Duchess of Lantia, you know, the new one? No one's really met her before, right? She took up the title, and the whole thing was shrouded in mystery." She hiccups, then crams another bite of Danish into her mouth while I sip my tea, waiting. "She sent a letter, I saw it last night, and she said she's coming to Wild Oak Woods for her first tour of the Lantian countryside." Her words are tumbling out of her, frantic to get out.

"Take a bite," I command, pointing at the Danish in her hand.

She does as I say, her cheeks full as a late-summer chipmunk's. "So—" A spray of crumbs leaves her mouth, and I wonder if maybe her charms are too strong, because that sort of lack of manners is not like Piper at all.

"Ahem." She blots her mouth again. "We're in between town leaders. Apparently, Hash left last night, so the letter came to me after it couldn't be delivered to him because I've lived here the next longest. No Hash Beauchamp, just me, and who decided I was the one to be in charge of this? And I was up all night baking, and stressed, and planning." The last syllable wobbles, her lower lip shaky. "And now it's up," *sniff*, "to me," *sniff*, "to make it perfect."

"Oh," I say, crossing my arms over my chest and glaring at her. "It's all on you, huh?"

"Exactly," she agrees, pouting.

"So what are the rest of your coven? What are the rest of your friends, the rest of all the amazing people and witches and creatures here? Chopped liver?" I stare pointedly at my arm. "That doesn't look like chopped liver to me. That looks like a hand attached to an arm that's perfectly capable and willing to help."

"You'll help?"

I make a deeply offended noise, my fingers clutching at my collarbone. "Why do you say that all surprised? Of *course* I will help. And I guarantee most of Wild Oak Woods will, too. This isn't all on your shoulders, Piper."

A crash sounds from downstairs, and I stand up so fast my chair falls backwards.

"Piper?" a deep voice yells, and Piper's hand flutters over her mouth in response.

"Is that—" I whisper, slightly stunned.

"Ga'Rek? I'm up here," Piper yells back. "I'm okay, I'm talking to Wren."

Fenn starts his demonic yodeling again and I cringe, stuffing the rest of the Danish in my mouth. If my ears are going to hurt, I might as well be calm and sugared up.

I take several long swallows of the tea. And caffeinated.

My apartment door bursts open, and the massive warrior orc ducks his head to clear the jamb, his eyes wild. Fenn goes quiet. Thankfully.

Black hair sticks out every which way, and I stare at him for a long moment.

He rakes a hand through it again, and it's obvious what's caused it to stand on end.

"Hi," Piper tells him softly.

"You scared me to death," he booms.

Fenn yaps at him, but the orc doesn't even glance away from Piper's puffy face.

"Who did this to you?" he asks, crossing the room with thunderous footsteps, then kneeling at her feet.

I take a bite of the Danish, too riveted to look away.

Even kneeling, he's so massive that he's still at eye-level with petite Piper.

He frowns at her, his tusks enormous, then dabs at a lone tear on her chin. "Why are you crying? Are you hurt? Where is the fool who did this?"

"I'm worried about the autumn festival." Her voice is hesitant, her eyes wide and shining, and I take another bite of the Danish to keep from commenting on the obvious attraction between them.

Fenn, however, twitches his whiskers and turns to look at me meaningfully.

I dip my chin in agreement.

"What in the moon's name is going on up there? A damned party?" Caelan's voice drifts through the still open door, and Ga'Rek blinks and stands, then hits his head on my ceiling and decides to kneel again.

"We're up here," I call out needlessly, then stuff some more cheese Danish in my mouth.

Caelan strolls through the door, then pauses, stuffing his hands in his pants pockets as he takes in the scene before him.

Me with my face crammed full of pastry, the orc staring up at Piper with utmost devotion, and Piper, whose face is puffy and red from bawling.

"What in the—"

"She's stressed because the Duchess of Lantia is coming to town for the autumn festival and she thinks it's all up to her to make sure it goes well." It comes out a garbled mess, and I choke on the flakey pastry, but can't quite bring myself to care, thanks to the charm.

Caelan races over and thumps my back and I cough, then swallow again.

He glares at me balefully. "You're having a breakfast party and you didn't invite me?"

"Oh, please," I tell him, then pull him down for a crumb-covered kiss that leaves me breathless. "I missed you."

"And I you. I came over with news to share, but it appears I've been upstaged yet again."

"It is not all on your shoulders, Piper," Ga'Rek tells her. I start to stand up to find him and Caelan a mug, and maybe some plates, but Caelan puts a heavy hand on my shoulder and presses another kiss against my temple.

He moves fluidly, so elegantly, to the kitchen, finding two teacups and four plates.

And just like that, it's clear to see.

We fit together, him and me.

That simple gesture, just getting the cups and plates out for my unexpected guests, and my heart warms, tears stinging my eyes.

There's no cookie or spell in the world that could have made him do that unless it was specifically crafted to do so.

Caelan did that all on his own.

He picks out a raspberry tart from the basket and puts it on a plate for me.

"Why?" I manage, though I'm not entirely sure what I'm asking.

"Just to see you smile, little golden witch."

He sinks into the chair next to me and reaches for my hand like it's the most natural thing in the whole world.

"So she's coming, and I'm the person who's lived here the longest, and it's up to me to make sure it goes off without a hitch. Everything has to be—"

Ga'Rek brushes his calloused knuckles over her cheek and she blinks, her words lost to silence.

The raspberry tart crunches as Caelan takes a bite, and I bite my lips to keep from laughing.

"We will help you. Everyone will. I haven't lived here long, but I can tell this is a good place, full of good people who will want to help you, Piper."

"Better than a book," Caelan mutters, nudging me with his knee.

I clap a hand over my mouth, the urge to laugh stronger than ever.

"I'm sorry that you feel like this is all on you," Ga'Rek continues, completely focused on her, "but it's not. Not at all. Right, Wren?"

"Absolutely," I agree, nodding for emphasis.

"Where is the jeweler witch?" someone yells from outside.

Caelan casts me a dark look. "I would recognize that voice anywhere." He crosses over to the arched, stained glass window that looks out over the street as Ga'Rek continues to reassure Piper in hushed tones. "You've got an entire pack of dwarves out there," he tells me. "Do you want me to kill them?"

"What?" I explode, the tart forgotten. "Why would I want that?"

"Oh, I don't know, they're disturbing the peace. They could have woken you up." He looks outraged at the prospect.

I pinch the bridge of my nose. "That's not a reason to murder someone, Caelan."

He pouts. "Fine. Get dressed. I'll hold the wretches off."

"I was rude to them the last time they were here." I peek around his broad back, my cheek on his bicep. "I wonder what they want."

"Obviously, they want to work with you. You'll charge them triple," he demands.

"Oh, and who died and put you in charge?" I ask, poking him.

"Hash Beauchamp."

"He's dead?" Piper says, her voice hitting fever pitch again.

Fenn yowls.

The dwarves outside begin yelling and shoving each other.

"No, he's not dead, it's so much worse than that," Caelan announces with relish. "He was a Seelie fae the whole time. High court." He taps his chin. "Apparently, I signed the deed to the damned inn the moment I signed for the rooms we rented. Can you believe it?" He huffs in astonishment.

Outside, one of the dwarves lets out a ululating cry, brandishing an axe at another.

"I don't have time for their nonsense," I mutter, pushing past Caelan to the window. "Piper, come here, I'm no good at this kind of magic. I need your help."

"I knew I should have woken up Velvet," she says miserably.

"Stop, we have Fenn. And Caelan." I tilt my head at him. "You smell like magic," I say.

"Well, that's part of what I was going to tell you—"

"Later," I interrupt, pointing at the dwarves, who are now chasing each other around with various frightening-looking weapons. "I cannot deal with a massacre outside my store before it's even open."

"Oh yes, it would be terrible were that to happen outside of business hours," Caelan snarks.

I take his hand firmly and reach out to Piper, already gathering the spell, the one my mother taught me when I was a little girl and I haven't had use for in many, many years.

Fenn bounds towards me, stretching up on his hind legs, his paws at my hip.

Piper takes my hand, the magic from the three beings I love most in the world funneling into me in a maelstrom.

Caelan's power is wondrous, and I marvel at it before the sound of shattering glass pulls my attention back to the pesky dwarves outside.

"Aquavitae, aquamarine," I pause, forgetting the spell. "Shit. Do the thing we did with the cats when I was a little bean." I close one eye, hoping that's close enough, feeling the magic surge out of me.

As one, the dwarves outside scream, stricken.

Instead of the water I tried to summon, a pile of what appears to be horse manure has plopped down in front of my store.

Caelan raises an elegant eyebrow at me, grinning fiercely. "Shit, eh?"

"It wasn't supposed to do that," I say glumly.

"I'm going to go get Nerissa." Piper sprints out of the apartment, Ga'Rek hot on her heels.

"Well, it did stop them from bludgeoning each other," Caelan drawls, scratching his jawline.

"I covered the street in shit," I say, gesturing wildly. "I'm not a nature witch, I enchant *jewelry*. What was I thinking?!"

Caelan purses his lips and one of the dwarves begins cursing wildly, loud enough to wake up the whole town.

I clap a hand over my mouth, but this time, it's not enough to stop the hysterical laughter from streaming out of it.

CHAPTER THIRTY-THREE

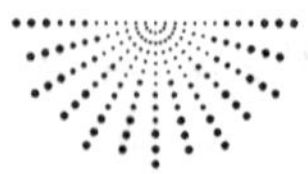

CAELAN

*N*erissa, the spellsmith witch, arrives on the scene and, to my discontent, does not laugh out loud at the sight of all the shit in the street. She reeks of dark magic, and the sensation of it prickles against my skin like needles.

"What do you mean, the inn is magic?" Wren asks for the tenth time.

I press the cup of tea I've brought her from her small apartment into her hands. "Drink."

She does as I say, guzzling the hot beverage like her life depends on it.

Good.

"The inn is old fae magic. I don't know how, I don't know what court…" I spread my hands wide. "Hash Beauchamp is a being that… defies everything I know about the Seelie Court."

Boner, who I brought with me and left sleeping in a basket downstairs, hobbles out of his makeshift carrier and lifts a back leg on the nearest potted plant.

"He left you his dog?"

"Yes, and my Boner appears to be leaking," I mutter. "I need to take that animal to a doctor."

"Rosalina is an animal mage," Wren says. "She'll be able to help him."

We stop talking, looking up abruptly as magic begins to roil around Nerissa, a dark cloud of shadow magic. Sparks crackle through the cloud, and the dwarves, stuck as they are in a pile of magicked shit, begin to try to free themselves in earnest.

My fangs lengthen, and I gently nudge Wren behind me, one arm clamped around her waist.

"It's fine, Caelan, this is what she does." A small hand presses into mine, and when I look down, Wren's eyes are the color of a calm sea and I breathe.

She's so perfectly mine, so perfectly her, and seeing her, holding her, makes me feel like everything is going to be alright.

I'm exactly where I'm supposed to be.

"Look," she says, jerking her chin at the street. "I'm safe. Nerissa wouldn't hurt me, Caelan."

My throat constricts at the thought of her being hurt, my heart throbbing in my chest.

"I expect we deserved that," a red-bearded dwarf calls out, looking suitably ashamed.

I harrumph.

"No one deserves what I did," my Wren says, slipping from my grip and walking towards the now clean dwarf. "I meant to dump water on you, just to shock you into not fighting. I'm so sorry." She shakes her head.

I simply can't believe I've mated to such a soft-hearted, gentle creature.

Soft all over, in all the right ways.

Maybe that's what I need, though. Something to dull the edges honed razor-sharp by a Dark Queen and my centuries in the Underhill.

Wren is exactly the witch to do that. I can't fathom my mate being anyone else.

"No, lass, I owe you an apology," the dwarf continues, a hand balancing on top of his axe.

"Wolf," a chorus of voices cry out.

I hiss, my fangs lengthening.

The largest wolf I've ever seen pads through the cobblestone streets, eyes glowing orange, grey fur coat dappled with white.

The sounds of steel being freed from sheaths ring out as the dwarves advance on the new threat.

"Stop," Wren calls out. I reach for her, but she evades me, running to the black-haired witch. "It's her familiar. It's her familiar."

The wolf pauses, pink tongue lolling out, and Boner limps slowly over to the newcomer. Slowly, the wolf begins to wag its tail and I exhale in relief.

"What kind of fucking witch has a wolf for a familiar?" one of the dwarves yells, and a few nod in agreement.

"A tired one," Nerissa says weakly, and the wolf trots over to her. She buries a hand in the beast's fur, leaning heavily on it. "You're welcome, by the way."

The dwarves are still standing there, weapons drawn, bristling with knives and axes, and in one case, a rusty, spiked morning star.

There's no accounting for taste, I suppose.

"Put your weapons away, you lot," the red-bearded dwarf cries out, waving a hand. "Leave the witch alone. Didn't you learn your lesson in the last shit storm?"

Grumbling, the dwarves do as he asks, and he turns back to Wren.

"I'm Lars Forkstone, of clan Rockhurst. We came to you this morning, our axes in hand, with the intent to apologize for our behavior."

"They want something," I say loudly, walking towards her.

Wren gives me a crooked smile that tells me she's already figured that out. Clever witch.

Lars grumbles, then points at me. "Your fae friend is right."

"I'm her mate." The words are filled with menace, and the dwarf raises his eyebrows.

"Well, that is something."

"He's my mate," Wren agrees, and I tug her close, inhaling her lovely scent, living for the way she melts into me.

"Good. We can use both of your help finding the dragon sapphire. We'll split it with you."

"Eighty us, twenty you," I interject.

Lars' ruddy cheeks go red. Redder, at least. "Forty-sixty," he counters.

"Seventy-thirty."

"Oh, stop it you two," Wren says, sighing. "Sixty-forty us."

"Aye, you've a deal." He holds out his big hand, and Wren shakes it.

"And you have to stay at my new inn tonight," I say blandly.

"That's not part of the—" he starts.

"We could do seventy-thirty if you don't want to stay with my mate," Wren tells him, batting her eyelashes.

"You need us to do the digging." Lars' brow furrows.

"You'll have meals prepared as part of your stay, included in the cost of your room," I tell him smoothly, a wicked grin on my face.

"He will?" Wren asks, disbelief widening her eyes. She clears her throat. "He will. You all will, I mean."

"We leave early tomorrow morning, at first light," I say imperiously.

"Aye, and do you know where it is?"

I smooth my hands over my shirt, slowly rolling up my sleeves, well aware our friend Lars is growing more irritated the longer I drag this out.

"As a matter of fact," I say slowly. "I do."

Thanks to Hash Beauchamp's—now my—inn, I do.

That's the funny thing about owning a fae building full of magic like the Old Wild Oaks Inn.

It has a way of knowing exactly what you need, and making sure you get it… eventually.

The shock on Wren's face turns joyous.

I pull her to me, planting a massive kiss against her mouth, claiming her for the whole town to see.

"Tomorrow morning," I tell the dwarf, keeping Wren against me. "We have plans today. I'll see you this evening at the old inn on Weeping Willow Way. You can't miss it."

They won't, either, not with the way the old place looks now: brand-new.

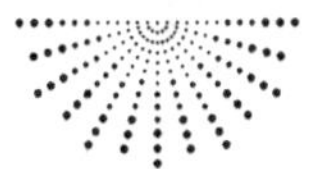

WREN

Caelan hums to himself as he puts his new dog back into the basket he apparently carried him over in.

"Hash Beauchamp is a Seelie fae?" I can't wrap my head around it. "You're sure?"

"He tricked me. The whole time, he tricked me." He shakes his head, sounding put-out but also impressed, as if someone fooling him is perhaps the most outrageous thing he's ever imagined.

"You said my house stank every time the brownie's shown up. Didn't Hash smell?"

"Well, yes, I smelled that wet dog odor as soon as I walked in the door of the place, but then Boner appeared, wet, limping, and absolutely foul in every way." He slips into a high-pitched baby voice, and my eyebrows shoot up as he boops the dog on its admittedly wet dog nose.

"I just can't believe it."

"I've noticed," Caelan says drily, then nudges my ribs with an elbow. "You aren't excited about the sapphires? And that I found out where they were? Don't you want to know? How are you not dying to know?"

"Of course I want to know, but…" I trail off, eyeing the panting, wheezing dog in the basket now hanging on Caelan's arm. "Frankly, I think we need to get that dog to Rosalina as soon as we can."

"Oh, I don't know," Caelan hesitates, then rolls his eyes, giving up. "Fine. I have a theory as to what's actually wrong with Boner, other than being limp, but I am open to what the Wild Oak Woods animal mage has to say." He licks his lips, and I impulsively pull his face down to mine, kissing him again.

"Fucking love the way you taste, little witch," Caelan growls, his fangs sharp against my mouth. "But my Boner needs help."

I burst out laughing, then raise one eyebrow and smooth a hand down the hard bulge in his pants. "I can see that."

He groans, capturing my mouth in his again… until a loud whistle makes my cheeks blush.

I pull away from him, laughing as I push one hand against his chest. "What were the plans you had in mind? The ones you said we had, you know, the ones I wasn't included in making?"

A bubble of happiness expands in my chest with every word. He made plans for us.

For us.

"Well," he says slowly. "The plan's now changed slightly, but you know what? I think it will be even better in the early evening." He takes my hand in his, pressing a soft kiss against my knuckles, his glacier-blue eyes drinking me in. "I can't keep you up too late," he finishes, his words full of meaning and heat.

"First, we'll take care of my dog, then I want to show you the inn." His eyes sparkle as he mentions his new project, and I can tell he's beyond excited to show me around. "We can have lunch… and then I thought we'd take a nap."

"A nap?" I laugh. "Why would you think I'd be able to sleep when there's so many other things we could do?"

Caelan steps closer, his mouth nuzzling against my ear, sending a shiver of excitement down my spine. "Because you'll need all your energy for what I have planned for you tonight."

My entire body clenches on nothing, and he laughs against my skin.

"Why am I not entirely sure what you mean by that?" I ask, pushing him away.

There's a completely wicked, lascivious look in his eyes, and I love that I'm the reason for it.

"Let's just say it's an ancient Unseelie fae tradition, my lovely witch," he murmurs, tracing a finger down my cheekbone.

"Is there a boner involved?" I ask, batting my eyelashes, adoring this playful side of him, so happy I'm the one that brings it out.

He tilts his head back and laughs, the sound so lovely it makes my heart leap, several people and creatures in the streets stopping to look our way.

I don't blame them one bit.

I'm addicted to the sound of it already.

❦

FAMILIAR FRIENDS IS a set of two small houses wedged together at the outskirts of town, a creamy white barn-like structure nestled next to Rosalina's pale sky-blue house and storefront. An owl sits on top of one of the open barn doors, looking for all the world like a statue used to scare off other birds.

Until its head swivels and it blinks two lamp-like eyes at us.

A white-spotted fawn snoozes under a tree next to Rosalina's barn, and a cat's curled up next to it, making biscuits on its hindleg, purring loud enough that I hear the animal before I see it.

Boner just stares vacantly around, his silvery cataracts likely obscuring his view of the rest of the animals.

We stroll into Rosalina's store, hand in hand, and Caelan pauses, looking around with an awe-struck expression.

I felt the same way the first time I wandered in here.

The front of Rosalina's house, where she conducts her business, is lined with large dark oak shelves stocked with all manner of animal food, treats, fresh-made medicinal ointments and poultices, as well as a collection of toys that rivals anything I ever saw in the northern city.

Pink fluff balls enchanted to float in front of playful cats, rechargeable with the right charm. An enchanted wooden rabbit for a dog to chase, never to be caught, always appearing back in the owner's hand when the dog gets too close. Exercise wheels for mice that create energy to be stored in a strange glass globe, crackling around the fragile perimeter when touched.

A trio of parrots hang on real tree branches suspended from the ceiling, a riot of blues and greens and deep reds, conversing in several different languages. Something thick and scaled contracts behind another chair, beady eyes and a forked tongue flicking out as the snake contemplates us.

A luna moth, larger than any I've ever seen before, sleeps on the door that leads to the rest of Rosalina's house.

It would be overwhelming, should be, even, were the animals all not so completely peaceful.

Fenn chirps before racing off to where Rosalina's mouse familiar is washing his face with careful pink paws, white whiskers trembling in excitement when she sees the fox, immediately swinging onto his fur and climbing happily on top of Fenn's head.

I let out an amused snort.

"Hey Wren," Rosalina emerges from around a corner, beaming at me. "And you must be Caelan. I've heard so much about you."

"From Squeak?" I ask, arching an eyebrow.

"My familiar loves to gossip," she agrees with a twinkle in her deep brown eyes. "But no, this was from a certain dog." Rosalina looks meaningfully at where Boner's snoozing in the basket.

"That's why we're here," Caelan says importantly, thrusting the basket onto a large table cleared off for the sole purpose of Rosalina's magical examinations. "My Boner has a limp."

I sigh, shaking my head, but Rosalina laughs. The sound cuts off abruptly as she swallows,

"He said you'd come in here and say something just like that."

Caelan goes still next to me. "Who?"

"Oh, an old friend." She picks Boner up off the table, stroking his head over and over again. "You called him Hash."

A faint hit of wild magic, nature magic, washes over me. It's as cold as an early spring rain, as fragrant as fresh-cut grass, the sweetness of honey on my tongue.

Boner barks, and I gasp.

The rheumy eyes, the silvery cataracts and drooling mouth are gone. So is the mangy coat, the too-long toenails, and the white muzzle.

"A fucking glamour," Caelan says in a low voice. "How did I not see it?"

"He told me you were coming, trickster," Rosalina tells him gently. "He said it was time to tame a trickster fae." She glances at me, her eyes kind, wise beyond the thirty years she seems. "He knew you would be well-suited for the task."

My jaw drops. "What?"

"Hash brought… her here? *My* Wren?"

His tone is so possessive, and it sends a girlish thrill of glee through me.

"He left her the store. He owned it, and when the last tenant left, he found you."

I have no words. "The Seelie fae brought me here?"

"They're watching you, Wren," she whispers, her voice hushed and serious. "They're watching all of us."

Caelan's hand tightens around mine, and he raises his chin.

"I'm sure we're *extremely* entertaining. I, for one, would have it no other way. But the question is, why?"

"If I knew why, I could have helped Hash with whatever plan he started putting in place."

The young dog, Boner, limp no more, wags his entire back half, licking Rosalina's cheek.

"Your dog, like you said, was glamoured to look old. Hash was too, and so was the inn. That's about all I know, that and things in Wild Oak Woods have never been exactly what they seem."

The hair on the back of my neck stands up.

"I'm not trying to scare you, Wren," she says, wrinkling her nose. "Or you, Caelan. I just… can't shake the feeling that—"

"Something's coming," I finish her sentence as we lock eyes.

She nods once, and Caelan clears his throat. "And you think Hash put me in charge of his… inn because of that?"

"He told me, when he last stopped by here with this dog—"

"Boner," Caelan interrupts.

I shoot him a look, shaking my head.

"Yep, that's the one," Rosalina continues smoothly, "that something was afoot in the Seelie Court. Something that could change everything."

Magic licks across my skin, a veritable storm cloud of power, and my magic, while strong, is nothing, nothing like that.

Rosalina inhales, her nostrils flaring, as she studies Caelan.

Caelan is emanating power.

"The Dark Queen took my power from me, bound me to her when I was but a child. I hardly remember having it, hardly remember anything from that day at all. That's the way of the Underhill." He gives a crooked smile, a fang flashing.

My heart aches for the boy he must have been. I can only imagine the pain of having a piece of yourself stolen away.

"The binding she did," Rosalina glances at me, "it broke the Queen's binding, didn't it?"

"No, but claiming her as my mate did." Caelan's grin turns

positively feral, a wild and beautiful thing. "You're right. So was Hash, the old bastard. Something is about to happen in Wild Oak Woods. The place he gave me, or I should say, tricked me into taking… it's more than an inn."

She leans forward; we both do, hanging on his every word. My skin prickles, an awareness of old magic at work, magic I don't understand, not really. My magic is measured in gold dust and gemstones and the spells worked into them. It's an ancient craft, sure.

But this?

This unbound power I feel creeping around the edges of my awareness, a movement in the periphery that's nothing when you go to look for it—it's something different. Something vast and terrifying and unknowable.

Boner barks, wriggling out of Rosalina's arms, heading back for Caelan at full speed. The dog licks his face, and he pats his head awkwardly.

Just like that, the power that looms all around us seems to suck back into itself, only a shadow of what it was remaining.

I frown. Maybe it was just my imagination.

Rosalina claps her hands together once and time speeds back up, that niggling sense of wrongness disappearing completely.

One of the parrots squawks, and a bristly hedgehog scuttles across the floor before disappearing into a wicker square in the corner.

"I'm sorry I didn't say anything sooner," Rosalina says, pursing her lips. "Hash had a way of making sure no one disrupted whatever plans he set in motion."

Her hands spread wide, an apologetic grimace turning the corners of her mouth down. "I don't know more than that. All I can tell you is that Hash means well, and that he wouldn't have chosen the two of you for any reason other than he thought you were the best suited."

"Best suited for what?" I explode, frustrated and more than a little scared.

Rosalina just gives me a sad smile and Caelan pulls me close to him, his hand smoothing across my hip, comforting and careful.

I relax at the touch.

I don't think I even realized how completely touch-starved I've been until this very moment.

"I don't know, Wren. I wish I did. But I do know that you coming here, Caelan and Ga'Rek and Kieran coming here… it feels like the start of something, doesn't it? The new coven, all of it." She shrugs a shoulder, that sad smile back on her face. "I don't know what to expect, only that change is on the wind."

Goosebumps pebble across my skin, a strange sense of foreboding making me swallow harder. "I feel it too," I say.

Caelan squeezes my hip, and Fenn's furry face nudges against my calf, his familiar weight on my foot.

"I'll protect you, no matter what," Caelan tells me fiercely.

"I hope it doesn't come to that," Rosalina murmurs, then brightens. "Here, I just got a shipment of chews and bones in. I bet Fenn and Boner would love them."

She bustles away, a parrot flitting from its perch to her shoulder, leaving Caelan and me in the relative silence of her store and alone with our thoughts.

CHAPTER THIRTY-FIVE

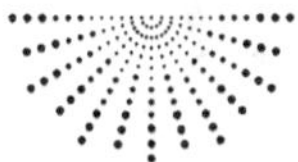

CAELAN

*H*ash Beauchamp's old inn isn't too far from Familiar Friends, further from the bustle of the downtown area of Wild Oak Woods and settled on the edge of the Ever Forest. Sprawling willows line the edge of the forest, boughs laden with delicate leaves swinging gently over the green grass.

"I think I should hang lanterns in those, don't you?" I ask, staring pensively at the edge of the forest. Beyond the willows, oaks and junipers fight for space, rose brambles in their last white bloom before autumn sets in. Their thick, thorny vines climb up trunks and cascade across the ground, making the Ever Forest nearly impenetrable.

"That would be lovely," Wren says, her cool hand tucked into my elbow.

Boner bounds ahead of us, his limp fully disappeared, chasing a bright blue butterfly.

"I'm worried," she says, then stops and stares.

"I won't let anything happen to you," I promise her. "You are everything to me."

"This… this is the inn?"

A laugh trips out of me, some of the burden of the knowledge —what little there was—that Rosalina imparted to us lightening at the shock and awe on Wren's face.

Fenn chases after Boner, his thick furry tail low behind him— he pounces on the dog, and the two of them roll around in the grass in front of the inn, yipping as they play.

"It's… wow."

I chuckle again, raising an eyebrow as I study the place. "That's how I felt this morning."

Gone is the sagging wood porch, in dire need of tearing down, more willing to be a bonfire than an actual structure. In its place, a white-washed stone patio, perfectly fitted together, no mortar needed, a hallmark of fae construction. Fluted stone columns hold up seven archways on the patio itself, mature coral and peach-colored roses climbing them.

The inn itself is full of high arched windows, stained glass depicting scenes from famous fables in the three largest that now look into the main room. More white stone forms the walls, lush plants dripping from artfully placed ledges.

"It's stunning. This is… this was here the whole time? I can't believe it."

"You should have seen my reaction this morning. Imagine waking up in a completely different room." I snort in amusement.

"How did none of us know it was glamoured the whole time?"

"I don't know. A town full of magical creatures, witches, and now fae, and none of us knew it was here. Whatever glamour Hash was able to cast, it was like nothing I've ever felt. And I thought the Dark Queen was the master of illusion." It irks me, in fact, that I had no idea.

I'd like to blame it on being so entirely distracted by the beauty on my arm, but I know, deep down, it's more than that.

I snap a rose off one of the climbing vines, and she blushes as I hand it to her.

"It's beautiful," she murmurs, raising it to her nose and inhaling deeply.

"It pales in comparison to you," I tell her, stroking my knuckles across the soft skin of her cheek. "Come on, let me show you the rest."

She laughs as I tug her up the stone steps to the towering doors of the inn, pulling one open and loving the way she gasps as she sees the interior.

The wooden floors gleam, a blond color that soaks up the multi-colored light streaming in from the windows. Luxurious furniture's arranged in comfortable groupings, and there are two stone fireplaces on either side of the grand room.

A long white table stretches down the middle of the room, with enough seats for half a hundred guests to take their meals.

Wren's speechless, a stunned look on her face as she takes it all in. Her jaw drops as she looks up, taking in the high ceilings and white stone rafters, the gleaming chandeliers and the fresh flowers.

"I grew up in magic, with magic all around, and I've never seen anything like this."

"I understand the feeling," I say, crossing my arms over my chest and watching her touch everything, her own witch's magic probing each new piece she finds.

"Show me the rest," she demands, and I bow deeply, making her laugh.

"As if I could tell you no," I tell her, kissing her temple.

Wren frowns adorably at that. "You can always tell me no."

"As if I didn't know that," I agree, and she rolls her eyes, grinning before her mouth twists to the side again.

"What?" I scrutinize her face.

"I need to… say something."

I tilt my head, waiting.

She nibbles her lower lip, and I groan. "When you do that, it makes me want to splay you out on this table and taste you all over."

Her brow furrows further.

Perhaps that was not the right thing to say.

I pull her into my arms, my heart hammering, sudden terror gripping me at whatever it is she's going to announce.

"I know I'm your mate, right?"

"Of course. I'm horrified you're even questioning it," I declare dramatically.

That, at least, makes her smile, chasing away the thunderstorm in her eyes. "I care about you, a lot. Already. But—"

My stomach falls, and I hardly dare draw breath.

"But I'm worried it might take me longer to feel the way you do, and I don't want you to be sad. Or decide I'm not worth it. Or decide waiting for me to give you my whole heart is taking too long. I don't want you to resent me."

It's my turn to stare, slack-jawed, at her.

"I'm so sorry," she mumbles, her hands fiddling with the ratty leather satchel she takes everywhere. "I don't want to hurt you—"

My fingers grip her chin, forcing her to look up at me. Her eyes brim with tears and I bend down, kissing her lashes and tasting salt on them.

"I will give you as much time as you need, my Wren, my golden witch. Simply sharing the same air with you is a gift. I don't need you to give me your heart all at once. I will savor every piece, every moment you deign me worthy of. I've waited for you a hundred years, two hundred… I'll enjoy pursuing you every minute you allow it."

"But—"

My mouth closes over hers, and I decide I can't wait until this evening to do what I want with her.

I pull away, my cock hard and ready for her already. "I know I said I'd want you to nap, but I'm afraid I need you do something for me now."

"Oh?" Her look immediately turns mischievous. "What's that?"

I hesitate, worried this will keep her from trusting me, keep her from needing me the way I need her, but I'm a selfish bastard, and I decide I don't care.

"I need you to run." It comes out a low growl, and I'm so fucking hard my balls ache with need.

"Run?" she whispers, eyes round and curious and so beautiful I want to memorize exactly how she looks right now. "Why? Is something wrong? What is it?"

"I need," I grit out, the urge so fucking intense it feels impossible, "to chase you. To claim you. In the old ways."

"Oh." Her eyebrows shoot up. "Oh. *Ooooh.*"

"That's right, little golden witch. I need you to run, and when I find you, I get to keep you." I bend down, biting her neck, not hard, but enough to make her gasp, and the scent of her arousal fills the air.

So fucking *good.*

"I…" She sounds so dismayed, so scared, and it's so at odds with the needy perfume of her cunt that I draw back, terrified I've hurt her, or worse, made her rethink our relationship completely.

She takes a few steps back from me, putting distance between us, her lower lip wobbling as she moves.

I want to pounce on her. I want to sink my fangs into her lush skin, mark her and knot her.

But I would despise myself if I scared her more, and I stand still, my legs trembling from the effort.

"I would like to see you try," she yells, and with that, she takes off, racing away from me with a high-pitched giggle that sets my soul on fire.

It takes me a moment to gather myself, to realize she's not afraid—she's excited, and she *wants* me to chase her.

I fucking *love* it.

"I will always find you," I swear to an empty room, but the inn hears me, and I get the feeling she won't evade me for very long.

CHAPTER THIRTY-SIX

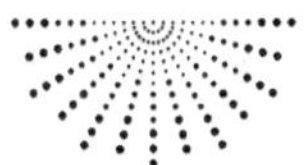

WREN

My hand's clamped over my mouth, my attempt to stifle slightly hysterical laughter not quite working. The curtain I decided to hide behind shakes with it, and I do my best to contain myself.

Who knew I'd love being chased so much?

He's hunted me through three rooms so far, always getting just so close, and then letting me go, allowing me to run away again.

The room I've chosen to run into now is lovely, decorated in shades of cream and cerulean, a huge arched window looking out over a garden I doubt any of us knew existed until today.

Hands grip my waist and I shriek, the noise turning to laughter first, then a moan.

"Mine," Caelan murmurs and kisses the base of neck, making me melt against him. He's hard against my back, and suddenly, I'm tired of running.

I want to be caught.

I start to turn around, to face him, but his hands keep me from moving.

"You like this, don't you, my Wren?"

Instead of answering, I squirm, trying to get away again, my heart beating so loudly I'm surprised it's not echoing off the walls.

Caelan hooks a foot around my shin, and I squeak as I start to fall. He catches me, holding my body tight against his so I can feel his heart, matching mine.

"You're not going anywhere, witch. You ran right into my room, and if you think I'm not going to knot you here all night, you're sorely mistaken."

His grip gentles, just slightly, and I go limp until he loosens even more, his hands gently wandering up my chest, cupping my breasts.

Then I let out a laugh as I succeed in breaking away from him.

I only take two steps before all the breath whooshes out of me, his arms like a vise around my chest, pulling my back against his chest again.

"Oh, is that how you're going to be, my love?" There's a feral edge to his voice that makes me tighten all over.

He holds me close, then rips my trousers with one strong yank.

"Hey, those are my favorite—"

"Your brownie will love to mend them for you."

"But what am I supposed to wear—" I gasp.

His hand slides into my underwear, between my legs, and he nudges my legs apart with a knee. "So wet for me already, lovely little witch," he purrs, and he's not wrong.

I suck in a breath, moaning again. My hips writhe against his hand, my body read for him.

"There she is, there's my lovely, lovely witch." His sharp fangs graze my throat, one hand massaging me so deliciously slowly that all the fight goes out of me.

His other hand runs up my shirt, finding my breast. I tilt my head as he nips at my skin, allowing him more access, allowing him all of me.

"So beautiful."

I preen under his praise, going near-limp as his fingers pinch my nipple, pleasure edged with pain. His fangs sharpen, and adrenaline spikes through me as I feel them elongate against the tender skin of my neck.

"Let me bite you," he growls. "Let me mark you as mine."

His hand moves upwards, tightening around my neck, his clever fingers circling my clit.

"So close," I say instead of yes.

"Oh, is that what my greedy, lovely witch wants? You want to come before I mark you? I have to earn it?" His fingers pick up the pace and I cry out, so close already.

"You need more, don't you, my love?"

I nod, at a loss for words. My entire being focuses on the sensations of Caelan against me, around me. His hard cock pressing into my back, his fingers playing me like a fiddle, his teeth tinging the pleasure with pain, somehow making it better.

Without warning, he thrusts two fingers deep inside me, his thumb strumming my clit like it was built for my pleasure.

"Tell me yes," he hisses, his breath hot against my skin.

"Make me come first," I tell him, practically pleading with him, my hips moving in rhythm with his hands.

His body leaves mine as quickly as he caught me, and I nearly fall backwards with the loss of it. In the next second, I'm airborne and he's carrying me to the sumptuous bed. His mouth covers mine, hot and needy, and I tangle my hands in his hair, wanting so much more.

The sound of fabric ripping startles me, and I harrumph as the offensive pieces of my shirt drift toward the floor, then claim his mouth in another desperate kiss.

"Fuck, Wren," he mutters, his hands gripping my ass. "Need to taste you."

He sets me on the bed, staring at me with worship in his eyes, and I've never felt more beautiful or powerful in my entire life.

"Take your clothes off," I demand, and point at the bed.

One side of his mouth kicks up in a cocky grin. "Ask nicely."

"Take your clothes off so I can suck your cock," I tell him, batting my eyelashes.

"Fuck," he moans.

"Please," I tack on, slightly desperate to watch him come undone, to taste and tease him just like he wants to do to me.

He does as I ask, finally, tugging his pants off while I do my best to pull his shirt off. Of course, that just makes it awkward, and by the time we tumble to the bed together, we're both laughing in each other's arms.

He kisses each cheek, then my nose, and when he reaches my mouth again, my whole body seems to sigh in relief.

Being in his arms feels like coming home.

It feels like a magic all our own.

CHAPTER THIRTY-SEVEN

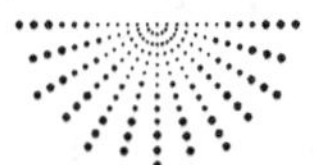

CAELAN

*W*ren surprises me, by turns demanding and submissive, keeping me guessing and keeping me absolutely wrapped around her perfect fingers.

When she pushes me down to the bed with a mischievous look, then doe-eyed innocence, I wonder if she'll ask me to beg for a taste of her.

I would do it in a heartbeat.

Instead, she kisses my stomach, lavishes attention on my nipples, making me hiss when she bites them.

"What was that for?" I huff a laugh.

"All's fair," she says in a sing-song voice, wrapping her slim hands around my wrists. I love the way she looks on top of me, straddling my chest, all peaches and cream complected against my lavender skin. Her breasts are the perfect mouthful and I bend forward, trying to catch one in my mouth, making her laugh.

"I love your laugh," I tell her, breathless with want and something so much better.

"Good," she whispers, grinning before leaning down and kissing me on the mouth. "I like that you make me laugh."

"That makes two of us. Now sit on my face so I can make you come. Then I'll mark you, and knot you, and the only noise you'll be making is that fucking fantastic groan while you come over and over again around me," I growl.

"Mmm," she says, tapping a finger against her chin. "Maybe."

I half sit up, outraged, and she laughs again, pushing my chest back down on the bed.

"What if I told you I had some ideas?" Those damned beautiful lashes flutter again, and I'm the one groaning, my cum leaking all over my stomach in anticipation.

"What if I told you I want you to act on them?" I snarl.

"Oooh, ask nicely." The little witch boops me on the nose like a bad cat.

I start to glare at her, and then she's turning around, showing me the perfect, creamy globes of her ass.

"That's a good little witch," I breathe and she settles on top of my mouth, her taste flooding my senses.

My hands go to her hips, holding her in place as I lick her, plunging my tongue deep inside her as she moans. I dig my fingers into her soft skin, desperate for her.

She leans forward, stretching long against my body, and before I can think straight, I'm raising my hips.

Her hot tongue darts out, licking the slit of my cock, and that's all it takes for me to come.

Pleasure blasts through me, and my toes curl as she continues to lap at my cock, her hands pumping up and down in a perfect rhythm.

I'm not sure there's much she could do that wouldn't be perfect at this point.

Perfect for me, at least.

"Well, that was unexpected," she says with a laugh as my cock jerks.

"Your turn," I growl, flipping her onto her back as she yelps adorably in surprise.

I set upon her with relish, flicking her clit slowly with my tongue, my own release allowing me patience with her.

She's ripe for me, wet and pink and glistening, and when I thrust my fingers inside her, her whole body trembles in response, her cunt clamping down on my fingers in a way that has me instantly hard for her again.

But she hasn't come yet, and I want to drag this out until she's as greedy for my knot as she can be.

I take my time, savoring her flavor, her little moans of pleasure, the way she begins to grind against my face.

"Caelan," she cries out, her hands covering mine on her hips. Her taste intensifies, and she bucks against me, deliciously wet and ready for me.

"There it is," I murmur, licking at her sweetness.

"Need you," she whines.

"I could never deny you," I growl, gently pushing her from my face.

Wren stares up at me desperately, her sex glistening, her nipples hard. Unable to resist, I nibble at one, and she lets out a stream of unintelligible praise, her head thrown back.

I take one more lick of her, then allow myself another, as a treat, before lining my cock up with her sweet entrance. We both groan as I rub it against her swollen clit, my knot forming around the base.

"Do you see how much I want you? Do you see the proof of what you do to me, my Wren, my love?"

"Please, please," she says, sweat shimmering on her creased brow, her eyes glassy with lust.

I grind my teeth, trying to hold myself back, trying to ease into her.

She whimpers as my cock slides into her, stretching around me. Inch by inch, I feed myself into her hot, wet cunt. I tremble, the need to slam into her outsized by the need to make this good for her.

Until her eyes fly open, and she glares at me. "If you don't knot me right now, you don't get to bite me."

I can't even laugh.

Instead, I unleash myself, slamming my cock deep inside her with one fucking fantastic thrust, my knot bulging as I rock my hips, working it into her.

Her fingernails dig into my ass, her eyes glazed, her cunt clenching gloriously around me.

"That's it, take all of me, Wren. You were made for me, my love. So tight and perfect."

Her back arches as the orgasm hits her, golden sparks shimmering around the room as her magic responds to mine, to me.

My knot pops into place and she shudders again, her legs shaking as she continues to come, milking my cock for everything it's worth.

I can't wait any longer.

"Let me mark you," I say on an exhalation. I want her to say yes, I need her to; I won't force it.

"Yes, I want it," she says, tilting her head.

I don't wait for her to change her mind.

I breathe her in, the perfume of her release, the scent of her gold-flecked magic, and I sink my teeth into her willing flesh.

She is mine, forever, no matter how long it takes her to accept me for her mate.

EPILOGUE

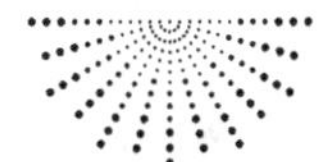

It takes two weeks for the dwarves and Caelan to locate the dragon sapphire vein. It turns out to be in one of the Ever Forest caves, and Caelan returns home to me covered in bramble scratches and dirt, a smug smile on his face and a cart loaded with raw sapphire, ready to be cut.

"Are you going to release me from my binding?" he asks, raising an eyebrow.

I laugh. "And risk you leaving my bed?"

His expression turns stricken, and I immediately regret the flippant joke.

"I'm sorry, I'm sorry, I love you, I didn't mean to hurt your feelings."

He freezes, his fangs the only thing moving in his moment of preternatural stillness, elongating.

Slowly, he beams at me, taking my hands in his. "Say it again."

"I'm sorry," I blurt, on the verge of tears. "I'm sorry, I didn't mean to hurt you—"

"Not that part, my love."

Realization dawns. "Oh," I breathe.

"Oh," he agrees.

A slow smile spreads across my face and I take a few running steps towards him, leaping into his arms.

"I love you," I repeat, marveling at it.

He beams at me, peppering my mouth with gentle kisses. "I know."

I scoff in disbelief. "That's not what you're supposed to say."

"I know you love me because you're mine, and I love you with every fiber of my being," he says, raising his brows. "Is that more like it?"

"Better, but I have some feedback for you."

"Oh?" he manages, laughing.

"Yeah, I think it would be more meaningful if you said it from between my legs."

"You little minx." He throws back his head, shaking with laughter. "You have work to do, golden Wren. Far be it from me to get in the way."

I pout as he sets me back down and grabs one of the wood crates out of the cart.

"I didn't break a sweat locating this and putting up with the surliest, rudest, most profane group of dwarves that ever burdened the earth just so you could skive off."

"Skive off?!"

"You heard me. You wanted the sapphires so badly you were willing to bind me to you, so now you get to show me what you can do with them. If you're a good little witch, maybe I'll reward you."

I sniff, trying to pretend like I'm not melting into a puddle from his lascivious promises.

"By the way," he says, carrying the heavy crate into the back door of my shop like it weighs nothing at all. "The Duchess is staying at the inn when she's here next week."

"Oh, I'm so proud of you!" I screech, clapping my hands together.

Of course, that sets Fenn off, and he starts his demonic scream as Caelan grunts, setting the crate down next to my work bench.

"Where else would she stay?" Caelan wipes his hands against each other. "The inn is the nicest place in town."

I nudge him with my shoulder, excited to work on the dragon sapphires despite my raging libido. You'd think getting knotted near nightly would dampen it a bit, but you'd be wrong.

Very wrong.

❧

THREE NIGHTS LATER, I have the first of the dragon sapphire gems cut, the last wax molded ring I made for it currently cooling, filled with rose gold and ready to be set.

The dragon sapphire's a deep teal, a bicolor beauty, and it took all my skill to cut a starburst design into the back of it.

It catches the light as it moves, sparkling, and I take a deep breath, ready to start chanting the incantation that will cause the wearer's speech to be twice as charming, or, if I'm lucky, four times as charming.

The starburst design on the back isn't just pretty. The additional cuts increase the surface area of the stone, giving the enchantment more room to permeate.

That is, in theory. It's the first time I've done such a thing, and a frisson of anxiety passes through me.

Four hours later, the stone is enchanted and my voice is completely hoarse, the sun rising through the front windows of the store.

A sound like a bell tinkling pulls me out of my magic-fueled stupor and I swivel around, expecting to see Caelan at the door.

Preferably holding a highly caffeinated beverage.

"Oh," I say, surprised. "It's you."

The brownie that's been keeping things under control at my house and store the last few weeks sits on top of a shelf, watching me with interested eyes.

"Not just my friend." The most beautiful voice I've ever heard sings through the air and I bolt upright, the sapphire forgotten in my hand.

A stunning fae woman stands in the middle of my store, graceful iridescent dragonfly wings at her back. Dark skin fades to a lovely pink at her wrists and ankles, and bells around both tinkle as she moves. Her hair falls in waves around her hips, her face so otherworldly perfect, splashed with silvery freckles, that I can hardly breathe, so overwhelmed that it brings tears to my eyes.

"Introducing Her Majesty, Queen of the Seelie fae," the brownie trills.

"You can call me Luna," the Queen says, waving a hand, a pink eyebrow quirked. "I'm not as formal as my sister under the hill."

I bow, then curtsy, getting caught somewhere in between as she laughs at me.

My nose scrunches up. "I've never met a queen before."

"Child, I don't stand on ceremony, no matter what our friend here thinks I should do." She tilts her head at the brownie, who's washing their head like a cat might.

"I've heard so much about you." She smiles, and it's like standing in the sunlight after a storm. "And I see I have not been misled." She glances down at the stone in my hand.

"Oh." Great. I've lost my ability to speak clearly. Maybe three all-nighters in a row wasn't the best idea.

"I would like to purchase that ring from you. In fact, I would like to offer you a job as a member of my court... at Wild Oak Woods, of course. We need you here, now more than ever."

I blink, unsure what she means by that.

"I would also like to commission a tiara. The thing about being queen is that I do get to have some fun, after all."

"A tiara," I repeat.

"Yes. Woven gold, dragon sapphires, protection spells."

"I can do that," I force out. "Protection against what?"

She gives me a cool look. "Against what's coming."

Right. Communication skills and the fae, apparently, are not acquainted.

"There," she points at my jeweler's bench.

Confused, I follow her gaze, and then my eyes widen.

A scroll, declaring me the chosen jeweler of the Seelie fae, along with an open box, gilded and gorgeous all on its own, full of coins. Enough to see me through the next two years.

"I trust that will be enough for a down-payment to start work?"

"Ah." I swallow hard. "Yes. Yes, it will."

"When can you finish the tiara by?"

I consider it, thinking of all the orders I don't have to get done because I don't have very many, thanks to the guild's rejection…

I have the blessing of the Seelie Queen.

My jaw drops as that sinks in.

I don't need the guild, not with this.

Tears begin to fill my eyes, gratitude nearly overwhelming.

"Don't cry, child. This is your destiny, and it might not be as easy as you imagine. I need the tiara by the winter solstice. Will that work for you?"

"Yes," I say immediately. "Thank you."

She smiles brightly at me, so lovely it hurts. In the blink of an eye she's gone, and my brownie too, leaving me alone with more money than I've ever seen in my life and a seal of approval that will, in fact, completely change my fate.

I only have one thought as I stare at it.

I can't wait to tell Caelan.

❦

THANK you so much for joining me on this journey to Wild Oak Woods!

For Piper and Ga'Rek's story, click here!

For a free short story about Lila and Druze, click here!

ALSO BY JANUARY BELL

FANTASY TITLES:

WILD OAK WOODS WORLD:

How To Tame A Trickster Fae

How To Woo A Warrior Orc

A CONQUEROR'S KINGDOM

Of Sword & Silver

Of Gods & Gold

FATED BY STARLIGHT

Following Fate: Prequel Novella

Claimed By The Lion: Book One

Stolen By The Scorpio: Book Two

Taurus Untamed: Book Three

SCIENCE FICTION TITLES:

ACCIDENTAL ALIEN BRIDES

Wed To The Alien Warlord

Wed To The Alien Prince

Wed To The Alien Brute

Wed To The Alien Gladiator

Wed To The Alien Beast

Wed To The Alien Assassin

Wed To The Alien Rogue

BOUND BY FIRE

Alien On Fire

Alien in Flames

ALIEN DATING GAMES

Alien Tides

ABOUT THE AUTHOR

January Bell writes steamy fantasy and sci-fi romance with a guaranteed happily ever after. Combining pure escapism, a little adventure, and a whole lotta love makes for romance that's a world apart. January spends her days writing, herding kids and ducks, and spends the nights staring at the stars.

For the latest updates, sign up for my newsletter by visiting www.januarybellromance.com, or follow me on Instagram and TikTok.